SKI-CROSSED LOVERS

LOVE ON THE PODIUM

ALLISON TEMPLE

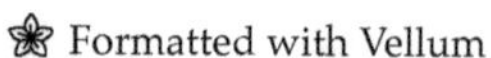 Formatted with Vellum

CONTENT WARNING

This book is pretty fluffy, but does involve a serious ski injury on the slopes, including mentions of blood, broken bones and other internal trauma, followed by a scene at the hospital. Also conversations about mental health. HEA still guaranteed though.

CHAPTER
ONE

Falling is part of skiing. From the first time I ever stood on a hill, I was taught that. I was maybe all of three years old, with a helmet that looked like a hollowed-out bowling ball, and a second-hand snowsuit that had been my brother's the winter before. I don't remember much from that far back, but I remember the howl of frustration that escaped my lips as I crashed to the snow for the fifth time that run. My legs were like wet noodles, bent at weird angles, and the heavy snow made it hard for me to swing the unwieldy skis around.

"Come on, buddy," the ski instructor said. "You gotta learn to get up on your own. You're always going to fall. It's part of skiing."

Looking back, that instructor was probably a bored nineteen-year-old who couldn't believe he'd been assigned babysitting duty on the beginner slope. So what did he know?

But he's right in that falling is inevitable. It just sucks when it happens in the Big Final of the last World Cup event of the year. Sucks extra hard when all I had to do was finish in the top three to qualify for the Olympics, and now I'll have to wait the whole off-season to earn my place.

I pick the snow out of my collar. The fall was a good one. The kind of yard sale that would make that old ski instructor pause the whole winding snow snake of kids to hike back up the mountainside and help child me collect myself and my gear, while calling me things like "kiddo" and "little dude" in the hopes of distracting me enough so I don't cry.

Crying's not an option now. Not with the world watching and the national team maple leaf on my chest. I get to my feet, waving my arms so the coaches and officials at the bottom of the slope know I'm okay. The other three racers are in the finishing area, cheering and high fiving each other. Austin's already got his helmet off, which makes him easy to spot with his long blond hair shining in the late afternoon sun. Did he win? He was ahead of me, but close enough I could have taken him in the last downhill section. Until Jean-Marie from the French team cut me off. Bastard. The last turn was tight, with the three of us trying to find the advantage that would put us ahead. The Norwegian was out of the running entirely. That is, until the final jump, where a gust of wind hit me while I was airborne. It was like an invisible hand grabbed my bib from the back and yanked on me so I landed off balance. I should have been able to catch myself. I've done it a million times before, in training and during races. But today just wasn't my day. I ate snow hard, and the other three left me in their tracks.

I love ski cross so much, but you never know how your day is going to end.

Once I've got my skis back on, I make my way to the bottom, so that at least my time will be officially recorded, even if I'm so far behind even the slowest skiers in qualifying I barely deserve to be there. Still doesn't stop Austin from throwing his arms around me like I won the whole thing.

"Zed! Did you see it?" he asks. He's smiling so hard his eyes crinkle at the corners like an old man's, which is saying something given that we both turned twenty-two last fall.

"Unless you mean did I see the snow caked inside my goggles, then no, man. I did not see anything." I'm not even wearing my goggles. They're pushed up on my helmet. But when I take them off and give them a shake, the lens is cracked. Jesus. That really was a good fall. Go big or go home. And it seems the best I've got is a chance to go home.

"I did it. Zed. Are you listening?" Austin's hopping up and down on his toes. The buckles of his rigid reinforced plastic ski boots rattle where he's loosened them after he was done his race.

"Yes, I'm listening," I say, even though I'm still examining my busted goggles. Good thing the season's over. Even the sponsors start to get antsy when you ask for your third replacement pair of something in a year. It's been a tough one. Every race has been the most important race of my life because each one is another chance to get closer to qualifying for—

Realization hits and I look back up at the big illuminated leaderboard.

1. GRIMM, A (CAN)

First place, Austin Grimm representing Canada.

Holy shit. Holy—

"Grimm!" I shout. "Holy shit, Grimm. You did it. You're going to the Olympics!"

Then we're hugging and jumping up and down and screaming. Someone slaps me on the back. I glance over my shoulder and it's Matthieu Girard. He came first in the Small Final earlier this afternoon, but it didn't matter. He already qualified at the meet two weeks ago in Switzerland.

"We're going to Cortina!" he says, and my heart swells. I grew up watching Matthieu race. This is his third games. He's been the Canadian ski cross champion six times in the last ten years, and always in the top ten nationally. Even being on the same team as him is the sort of thing that makes me wonder how this is my life. To be on the same Olympic team as him? Wild.

Only I'm not on the same Olympic team. Not yet.

He seems to have the same realization I do. Probably sees it on my face. I've never been good at hiding things. Never really needed to. I've known what I wanted since I was big enough to put on a pair of skis, and I knew the only way to make it happen was to work my ass off. To ski harder and train harder than everyone else. So many of the kids in my ski club were there to go fast and have fun. For some, that was even enough to get pretty far in the regional race circuits. Good for them. But I knew it was going to take more than goofing off to make it to this level. And when I met Austin? The race was on.

"Don't worry, Cedric," Matthieu says with another pat on the back. He says my name in the French Canadian way: Say-dreek. "There's still next season. That was a tough break today. You'll get it next time."

My ears turn flaming hot inside my helmet. Sometimes when Matthieu talks to me, I want to roll over and ask him to rub my belly, the way Luna, our old German shepherd, would do when you called her a good girl. But I'm not a dog. Or a kid. I'm a man with a serious ski career. My hero worship for Matthieu Girard will stay a secret until the day I die.

Even though he probably knows.

Austin's talking to a reporter, all smiles. Ski cross isn't exactly a high-profile international sport. We've got our own World Cup circuit, but when it comes to media coverage and sponsorships, we're a lot farther down the food chain than the alpine events like slalom, or even a lot of the other freestyle ski and snowboard competitions like big air and the half pipe. Still, we have a following, and I hope everyone at home sees Austin's excitement. He's had an awesome season, including a couple lucky podium finishes that no one expected early on. That's why he's qualified already. Matthieu is right. I'll get there. In our little duo, Austin's always had the raw talent and style. I've been the technician. But there's room for both on the Olympic team. Canada can send up to four athletes to the Olympics, and only two spots have been filled. There's lots of time to catch up next season.

"You should have given him more room on that last turn," Ivan says as he comes up to me. He's the Team Canada ski cross head coach. He won the Olympics in Lake Placid in the downhill. That was like twenty-five years before I was born. He's a grumpy bastard who never says anything nicer than "Do it faster next time" and "I told you to stay low in the turn," but most of the time he's right.

I hang my head. "I know. But we were side by side. No one had right of way."

Ivan purses his lips. His sunglasses are on the top of his head, and the tan lines around his eyes and at his temples talk about decades spent wearing them while sunlight reflects off the snow. Most people don't know you can tan in winter. Probably because if you live in the parts of Canada (i.e., most of them) where winter is spent with a scarf around your face, a toque squished down over your eyebrows, and a sun that never actually breaks through the endless days of grey cloud cover, you're almost definitely also vitamin D deficient. But if you live your life on the mountains, above the cloud line and where the air is thinner, you can look like you just walked off the beach all year long.

"You'd have made up the time," Ivan says, ignoring my excuse. "Instead you fell. So which was the right call?"

Before I can answer, Austin finishes his interview and swaggers back towards me, arms swinging by his sides to keep his balance in his hard boots on the soft snow. I drop to my knees, holding out an imaginary pen.

"Mr. Grimm. Please, Mr. Grimm. Can I have your autograph? Is it true you're going to the Olympics?"

At my display, Ivan shakes his head and walks away. I'm a lost cause for now. He can have all of the off-season and next year to remind me why he's the coach and I'm the lowly athlete.

Austin laughs, rolling his eyes. "Shut up, Zed."

"No, really," I say, rocking back up to my feet. "You're my hero, Mr. Grimm."

He punches my arm, shaking his head, but his smile never fades. The late afternoon sun shines off his skin, turning the five o'clock shadow on his jaw golden. He's beautiful. A golden boy with a gold medal. Not an Olympic one, but a World Cup medal is pretty special too.

Austin and I met when we were nine. Until he joined the ski club, I was the fastest kid on the team. But the very first day, he smoked me on the run, leaving me to eat his snow. That pissed me off. I didn't like being second. For a few weekends, I swore Austin Grimm and I would be mortal enemies for the rest of our lives. But then one afternoon we were doing cat-and-mouse drills, practicing passing each other. In a minute where we were watching other kids doing the same, Austin whispered, "I wanted you to be my partner because you're the best skier here," and my conviction that I would hate him until I died turned almost immediately to respect for his superb observation skills. We were best friends by Christmas, and we've had each other's backs the whole time we worked up the junior alpine circuit, before moving over to ski cross right around the time we finished high school.

As I watch Austin step up onto the top level of the podium and hold his hands up in triumph, all I can think is that we planned for this. More than dreamed. We worked our asses off. Other people would have decided to be rivals. And don't get me wrong. I love nothing more than beating his ass in a race. But what I want more than anything is for the two of us to stand on top of the podium together while they play "O Canada." I mean, obviously one of us will have to come in second, but most days I don't even care who it is. If I'm going to lose to anyone, losing to Austin at the Olympics is pretty much the dream. Aside from winning gold, of course.

When the ceremonies are done, and the last of our gear is handed off to the equipment team, Austin and I board the bus back to the resort. This weekend's competition was in Maine. The conditions were touch and go, with the milder temperatures of the late season making the snow soft and prone to grabbing your edges at the worst possible moment.

"That was so incredible," Austin says, practically shaking with excitement as we ride the elevator back up to our shared hotel room. Accommodations were cozy this weekend, but at least the room has two beds, and they were paid for by Canada Ski. Back when we were coming up, doing junior racing and even on the NorAm Cup circuit, accommodations were often self-funded, which led to a lot of nights spent squeezed with too many bodies in a king-size bed if you were lucky or—if you were less fortunate —on the floor or, once, with a nest of pillows and blankets in the bathtub.

"The Olympics!" Kage says, gaze going dreamy. He's the newest member on the team and just turned nineteen. He's got a lot of raw talent, but hasn't quite figured out how to put all the pieces together at the senior national level. "That's so cool."

Austin's smile gets bigger. "We should celebrate! Go out tonight. Nothing to do tomorrow but the photoshoot with Apex."

We all groan simultaneously. Me, Austin, Kage, Matthieu, and Andrew Spinner, who makes up the fifth person on the men's team. Like Matthieu, he's a veteran and the two of them tend to keep to themselves. Probably say things like "young whipper-snappers" and "back in my day" when we're not around.

So I'm surprised when Matthieu says, "A celebration would be good."

"But the photoshoot," I say. Not that I'm looking forward to it. It's a necessary evil. Someone's got to pay for the hotel rooms after all, and sponsors expect a certain quid pro quo for their generosity. But we're athletes, not models. I'd rather do an extra weight session in the gym than smile for the camera.

Spinner huffs a laugh. "You can ski hungover. Trust me."

Austin smacks my shoulder, making me jump. "Come on, Zed! Let's do it." His eyes sparkle with an electric energy that I'm surprised isn't making his long hair stand up on end.

"There's karaoke," Kage says. "I heard some of the race volunteers talking about it. Supposed to be a fun time."

The only thing I want to do less than a photoshoot is sing karaoke. Trust Kage to find out about the local nightlife. He didn't make it out of the qualifying runs this weekend. The first day of ski cross is timed runs, with only the top thirty-two advancing to actual competition the following day. Kage finished in the low forties, which means he's had lots of time to sit around the hill and find out where all the local dive bars and cheesy karaoke nights are held.

Still, I groan. "Guys, I don't know." Usually I'm up for at least a couple drinks, but there's a knot in my hip that needs a hot shower and some vigorous massage. "I'll probably chill tonight." I can stretch it out. Ivan will send out footage from the races. I can watch them and figure out where things went sideways today. Besides the close turn with the Norwegian and the hand of god pulling on my bib, I mean. There are always places for improvement in every single race.

"Zeddy," Austin says, pushing out his lower lip as he wraps an arm around my waist and rests his chin on my shoulder. "The season's over. Let's relax. We've got all summer to train."

I go to point out that's easy for him to say, since he's already qualified for the Games. Same with Matthieu. Some of us have to work even harder over the next few months. There are five of us and only four spots to go to the Olympics. With two of them spoken for, my chances are getting slimmer.

But they're all watching me expectantly. We're off the elevator and standing in the hall. I get the feeling if I don't commit, they'll all follow me to my room. Maybe even into the shower.

I sigh. When I say, "Fine. Let's do it," the others cheer ecstatically. My legs ache as I stagger to my room to change. I really would prefer to stay in tonight. With Austin in the games, all pressure is on me to qualify too and reach our goals.

But one night of fun won't hurt.

Will it?

CHAPTER
TWO

SOMEHOW, by the time the sun sets and we're all showered and changed, the plan has grown into an unofficial team-wide event. The women's team comes too, along with a significant chunk of the support staff. This is turning into a full-fledged party.

We pile into a bunch of cabs to head out from the resort. Like most ski towns in the northeastern US, there's not much here. Post office, a few banks, new trendy craft breweries that close at ten because that's when the families who actually make up their whole clientele have gone home for the night. But at the end of one street where the sports shops and souvenir places give way to things like a dentist's office and a bakery with a faded sign is a shabby looking bar with neon beer logos in the windows and the mixed smell of booze, sweat, and oil from a deep fryer that probably hasn't been cleaned this year that greets us as we walk through the door.

I love places like this.

My earlier fatigue and serious mood fade as we're greeted by shouts from more friends, while a woman on the small platform that functions as a stage at the far side of the bar sings a pretty decent version of "Firework" by Katy Perry. People flip through tattered binders, looking for their next hit at the karaoke machine.

"What are we going to sing?" Austin asks as he slings an arm over my shoulders. He's still got the same feverish energy from earlier. He can't seem to stand still and flits among our teammates and even chats up athletes from other teams who are here tonight. I'm happy for him, obviously. He's had the best day of his career and he's allowed to be excited about that. But when the adrenaline wears off, he's going to crash so hard.

For now though, the whole bar is full of skiers and snowboarders from this weekend's races, all looking to blow off some steam and enjoy a night on the town. There's maybe a couple locals too, but they're outnumbered by people I've seen all weekend and pretty much at every other event for the last few years. The mood is loud. It's a party, after all. Win or lose, the season is over and it's time to let loose, even though we all know training will start again as soon as we get home.

The beer flows freely. Matthieu buys the first round. Kage gets carded at the bar and sulks when the bartender makes him put on a bright yellow wristband so all the staff know he's underage.

"I'm nineteen," he pouts. "That's legal at home."

It's legal pretty much anywhere on the World Cup circuit, but American laws around drinking are almost as weird as their laws around pretty much anything else. Matthieu orders him a ginger ale.

"Better luck next year," he says.

Austin signs us up to sing "Pour Some Sugar on Me." The whole team gets up. Skiers, riders, even some of the techs, trainers and coaches who have come out. We're close to twenty-five people. Most spectators don't realize a ski team has so many members who never compete. Coaches, strength trainers and physiotherapists. A whole separate entourage who are only responsible for maintaining our equipment. We even have two team sports psychologists, though they don't travel with us unless it's for a really big event like the Olympics.

The Olympics . . . I have to make it. Now that Austin's in, if I don't go too . . .

Austin throws an arm around me again, holding the mic under my mouth as he winks and prompts me to sing. I didn't mean to get distracted. The whole point of being here is to have fun, not mope and make plans. Our song is terrible. Too loud, and someone on the other side of the group doesn't seem to understand the concept of carrying a tune. It sounds more like they're tripping down a long and bumpy flight of stairs. But whatever, we all have a good time.

The crowd cheers when we finish. Two women from the American team get up next, pouring their souls into a song I don't know and making me very glad I'm not the man they're singing about. He sounds like an absolute dick who deserves everything they say they're going to do as their voices fill the bar. Austin and I get a few more beers.

"To the Olympics!" Austin says, holding his drink up in salutation. I make myself smile as I toast his achievement. He's worked hard for it. I know. I've been there every step of the way. The wins, the losses. When he broke his arm in a fall two years ago and spent six weeks in a cast, then a few more weeks on limited training before the doctors cleared him. He was a miserable bastard for that whole two-month period. We've spent our entire lives learning to do one thing better than ninety-nine percent of all the other people in the world, and when we can't do it, everything sucks.

I start to relax. Nothing sucks right now. The beer is surprisingly good for yellow American lager. The karaoke is terrible, but that's kind of the whole point of karaoke. There are a few ringers who clearly have their songs picked out and perfected ahead of time. And there's also a lady who must be local and has had an awful lot to drink tonight because she keeps going up to sing old Billy Joel songs my dad likes. Every time, she pauses in the middle to say things like "You're all so wonderful" and "Thanks for coming out tonight" like we're an audience to her solo lounge act and not mildly drunk international athletes patiently waiting for her to get off the stage so someone fun can step up.

As a couple of Australians have the gall to get up and attempt "House of the Rising Sun," I realize Austin's not sitting next to me anymore. Bathroom, probably, but as I let my gaze move over the crowd, I spot his blond hair on the far side of the room. He's chatting with a couple of the skiers from the French team. They're all holding drinks and raising them in a toast. We may all be rivals on the snow, but here, a little camaraderie isn't unexpected. One of the Frenchmen wanders away, leaving Austin to talk with the remaining one, whose name is Daniel. I don't know him very well, and what I do know I don't like, but he and Austin seem to be on better terms. He says something and Austin laughs, head tipped back. Daniel smiles and pushes his chair a little closer. Austin's smile doesn't falter as he leans in to hear something Daniel says, mouth very close to Austin's ear.

A tight feeling squeezes my chest. It wouldn't be the first night one of us found some company to take back to the hotel. All that intensity and concentration from the weekend needs an outlet, after all. But they damn well better not go back to my room, even if it's Austin's too. That's bad form. More than once, I've returned to my accommodations after a late-night training session or chat with one of the coaches to find a pair of goggles slung over the doorknob. The generally understood symbol for "come back later." Normally I'm fine with it, but something about Austin's jittery vibe tonight says it won't be a quick in and out with dear old Daniel. They could go for a while.

Or maybe not. They're busy having their literal tête-à-tête, and at one point Daniel even puts a hand on Austin's knee, which he either doesn't notice or mind. But then the hand moves, sliding up the inside of Austin's thigh, and he jerks, standing up straight. His expression turns from happy and maybe a little drunk to confused. He speaks again, but his smile fades. Daniel says something in return, and Austin shakes his head, turning to go. Except that doesn't seem to be part of Daniel's plan, because he grabs Austin's sleeve and pulls him back.

I'm moving across the bar before I even make the decision. Austin and Daniel's conversation turns heated. Daniel's a couple inches taller than Austin, and he never lets go of Austin's flannel. His mouth turns into a hard line as he spits tight words in Austin's face. When his free hand starts to wander below Austin's belt for a second time, Austin struggles to get free, but all he succeeds in doing is knocking over a stool at the table behind him. The crash makes people turn, which at least forces Daniel to let Austin go. It also gives me enough time to reach them.

"Hey, buddy," I say, fixing a smile on my face. No need to escalate things if I can get us both out of here with a little friendly chit-chat. "Everything okay here?"

"Of course," Austin says, righting the stool. The people around us have already lost interest and turned away.

But Daniel sneers. "What's your boyfriend doing here?" he asks in his prissy French accent. I grew up near Ottawa and have always preferred the French-Canadian one. It's solid. Familiar. People from France sound like they only know how to use the very tip of their tongue and lips, not their whole mouth and throat.

Austin has always had terrible taste in men.

"Just coming to offer you both another round. Beer for everyone?"

More sneering. "I do not drink American beer."

I roll my eyes and wave my hands, making it clear I do not give a fuck.

"I can see if zey have some white wine," I say in an exaggerated version of Daniel's stick-up-his-ass intonation.

"Go away, Cedric. I don't do threesomes either." He pushes me aside, reaching for Austin. Regardless of whether he drinks beer or wine, he's drunk. Drunker than either of us. Doesn't matter what he consumed to get there.

"I think I've had enough for tonight," Austin says, batting his hand away.

"No," Daniel whines. "We were having a nice time." He presses the advantage of his height again, trying to back Austin up against a pillar.

"Listen," I say, grabbing Daniel's shirt, but he rounds on me violently and I get zero warning before his fist collides with my face.

Jesus Christ.

I've never been punched before. I'm a skier, not a hockey player. The impact is enough that my vision and hearing both blank out for a second as I drop to the ground like a sack of potatoes. Someone shouts, and when I can see and hear again, Austin is standing over me, and the rest of my team must have received some kind of maple-scented bat signal, because Matthieu, Spinner, Kage, and everyone else are pushing through the crowd. Unfortunately, Daniel must have also sent up some high-pitched frequency that only the French can hear, because he's got reinforcements coming too.

I've never been in a bar fight before. Don't really feel like changing that tonight. I scramble to my feet. Or I try, but my feet keep skidding out from under me on a floor made slippery from snowy boots and a few spilled drinks. Then strong arms lock around my waist and hoist me upward. I start to fight them off, until I notice the plaid shirt around the arm and my next round of self-defence dies. Because it's Austin. I stop struggling and instead get myself turned around, keeping low as we duck and weave our way through the angry crowd. Hopefully, with us out of the way, cooler heads will prevail, but I don't want to wait around and see. I stay close to Austin and eventually he leads me down a narrow hall and out the back door into the chilly evening.

"What the fuck was that?" I say, panting as my breath turns to white vapour clouds.

"What the fuck did you think you were doing?" Austin shoves me backward, but while there's a spark in his gaze, his words have an edge of laughter to them that says he's not angry so much as hyped up.

"What the fuck was *I* doing? What the fuck were you doing? Flirting with Daniel? Seriously? That guy has always been an asshole." He cut me off at a meet in Val d'Isolde last year. It was so blatant I even filed a protest with the officials. They eventually disqualified him and I moved up to fifth place. I don't think he's ever forgiven me.

"I wasn't flirting," he says, sounding genuinely confused that I would even suggest it.

"He certainly thought so. He was all set to give you a hand job right there in the middle of those two women singing Taylor Swift."

"And I told him no." His eyes narrow unexpectedly. "I don't need you coming to my rescue."

"Of course you do. Someone has to save you from ze handsy Frenchman." I do the last part in Daniel's stuck-up accent again, which makes Austin laugh.

"Don't be dramatic, Zed." Austin puts a hand on my face, brushing over the same spot Daniel punched just a few minutes ago. It throbs so much my eyes water. "Does that hurt?" he asks, voice getting soft.

"What do you think, dumbass?" I poke at it too, wincing at my own touch, which is much less gentle than Austin's. I don't think anything is broken, but it's swelling. Goddammit. We even have that photoshoot tomorrow. Tara's going to kill me.

"Let me look at it," Austin says, backing me up until my heels hit the wall. It's like Daniel with the pillar, except there's no aggression. Only concern. Gently, he touches the lump on my cheek again.

"Your fingers are cold," I whine.

"They are not." His brow creases. "Shut up. We were inside five seconds ago."

"Let go," I try to pull free, but he grabs my chin, holding my face in place so our gazes lock. The air around us is changing, and something under my clothes warms. We're all alone out here, with only the occasional rush of a car passing on the other side of the building and the muffled sound of music coming from inside the bar.

I lick my lips. A voice in my head says I need to get out of whatever is going on here. Not that I'm in danger, but we're standing on the edge of something and one good push will have us tumbling over the edge.

I go for humour, hoping to defuse the growing tension.

"If you're going to be all Papa Bear, the least you could do is kiss it better."

His fingers tighten on my chin. Alarm bells sound in my head. Austin's face goes deadly serious, and I hold my breath as he gets even closer than he was a second ago. I jolt when his lips brush over my cheek. Once. Twice. I'm holding my breath and suddenly, even if he released his hold on me, I don't think I'd squirm away.

"Better?" he asks, voice turning rough.

"Uh. Yeah. Thanks."

He's so close there's no room for light between us. Just a waft of his breath before his lips move from my cheek to my mouth. He hovers for a second, and even if we aren't touching I can feel him. Feel how close he is. I close my eyes and let what's about to happen finally happen.

He kisses me. For real this time. Lips on mine, warm, soft, then firmer as he moves over my mouth, asking a silent question that we've never dared to ask each other before.

We have been best friends since we were nine. I came out before he did. Some of our teammates have joked how there's no way we've never hooked up, but it's true. Austin is my best friend. My brother on the snow. Why the hell would I risk fucking any of that up for an orgasm when there are plenty of willing bodies on any given race weekend? Austin's not the only one to hang those goggles on the door for a few moments of privacy.

But now he's kissing me. He's taking the risk. Seems like the least I can do is risk with him. It's not like I've never thought about kissing him. Just haven't acted on it when safer options were available. Now, though, I pull him in, grabbing fistfuls of his shirt.

There's nowhere to move with the wall behind me, but he crowds up against me, pressing his whole body against mine until I don't feel the cold air anymore. We're more than kissing now. This isn't only about making me feel better after getting punched by a dickhead. I keep tugging on his shirt, trying to find any little inch of space that needs filling, until he finally catches my wrist and lifts my arm over my head and shit, that's hot. He runs his lips over my cheek and down my jaw. His hips press against mine and holy hell. I groan, finally letting go of his shirt so I can wrap my hands around his ass and rub against him. My dick is already getting hard in my jeans, which is wild because it's *Austin*. I've never truly considered this could be a possibility. Never seriously imagined him while I—okay, that's not true. Because at the end of the day we're dudes who like other dudes—or in Austin's case, dudes and also the ladies. And there were definitely nights when we were teenagers who only thought about skiing and sex—even though neither of us had ever actually had sex at that point— where Austin tried to hide his soft whimpers as he jerked off under the covers in the hotel room bed next to mine. And maybe I jerked off too while I listened to him.

My hips roll, thrusting my already aching dick against my fly. Against him, and the hard length that's formed inside his pants too. He groans, pinning me against the hard concrete.

"Austin," I gasp. This is so much better than any awkward late-night wank into a thermal sock.

Unfortunately, saying his name breaks the spell we are both falling under. He stumbles back like he's the one who's been punched now. He's breathing hard, and he looks at me like he's never seen me before.

"I-I shouldn't have done that. Not yet," he says.

Not yet? Then when? And why not now? Because it turns out kissing Austin is pretty much the best thing ever, short of standing on that podium at the Olympics while they play the national anthem and I know that everyone is watching me.

But before I can say anything about any of that, Austin shakes his head a final time, then spins and runs away like he's being chased. Runs! One second, he's got me so turned on I might be convinced to come in my pants. The next, the cold wind blows through me as I shiver alone in the dark.

THERE GOES MY NIGHT. I return to the bar, but everything is back like it was. Someone's singing Olivia Rodrigo terribly, and Kage and Matthieu are right up at the edge of the stage, cheering like they're watching Olivia herself. There's no sign of Daniel or any kind of fight or altercation or whatever even happened after Austin and I got out of there. Just like there's no sign of Austin. The only proof I have that any of the last few minutes occurred the way I think they did is the welt on my cheek and the way my chin stings in the places Austin's stubble scraped over it a moment ago.

When I go back outside again, the parking lot is dead silent. Where the hell did he go?

And why the hell did he kiss me?

I put my hand to my lips, reliving the feeling of his mouth on mine. The hungry sounds he made as he tried to get even closer to me. What the hell? This is even more confusing than some random drunk Frenchman punching me instead of taking the loss and finding someone else to grope.

But where is Austin? He can't have gone running off into the night. It may be late season, teetering on spring, but it's still below freezing now that the sun is down and he didn't even have a coat.

I text him.

Hey? Are you okay?

Where did you go?

I'm still at the bar. We don't have to talk. Just let me know you're safe.

It's a long way up some very dark roads to get back to the resort. He couldn't have done it on foot. But he doesn't answer me either.

I wait outside until I'm shivering, thinking he needed a second to himself. But after another twenty minutes, he still hasn't returned, so I retrieve my jacket from a pile we all made in the corner of one booth when we walked in, then grab Austin's too.

I'm going back to the hotel. Tell me when you get in.

The whole cab ride up the mountain road, I keep an eye out for Austin trudging in the dark but never see him. I text a few more times, but they all go unread. I think about calling Matthieu. Maybe even Ivan. But Austin is a grown-up and calling the others feels like tattling on him. Plus I'll have to tell them what happened after we left the bar. We got teased enough when we first joined the team. Were we friends, or were we *friends*? Some people will be absolutely insufferable if they hear about the two of us kissing behind a sketchy karaoke bar in the middle of the night.

When I walk through the heavy doors into the hotel lobby, Austin is sitting in one of the overstuffed chairs.

"I'm an idiot," he says when I approach him.

I snort. "That's not news." He's my best friend and I would do anything for him, but Austin's always been the chaos gremlin in our little pair. He skis on instinct. Makes decisions on the fly. Most of the time that works for him. Works for us. He dreams big and I come up with the plan and execute. But right now, I need him to come back to earth so we can talk.

"I shouldn't have run away like that."

That's probably as close to an apology as I'm going to get, so I say, "Yeah, that wasn't a great choice."

But we're both still clearly skiing on different terrain, because he says, "My room key was in my coat."

Oh. And here I thought we were going to have an adult conversation about what happened back there.

"Jesus, did you run all the way up here?" I wasn't that far behind him. We may be well matched on skis, and Austin's always been able to outrun me, but for him to make it the whole way without me overtaking him in a literal car seems impossible.

"I needed some air. Clear my head." He shivers. When I grab his hand, it's like ice.

"Come on," I say, pulling him to his feet.

"Where?" he asks. He still won't quite look at me.

"Upstairs." To our room which, right now, is a less-than-ideal situation if he's going to continue making this uncomfortable, but whatever. I'll make sure he's okay, then we can both crash. This whole night has been weird. Better to bring it to a close now that I know everyone's safe.

Yet as soon as the elevator doors shut, Austin rounds on me, once again backing me up against the wall. He lingers there, mouth an inch away from mine. The tip of his nose brushes my cheek and even that's cold.

"I really want to kiss you again," he says, voice rough. "I should probably tell you I've been wanting to kiss you for a while now."

My brain goes blank. What am I supposed to say to that? He's my best friend. We tell each other everything. Exactly how long is "a while," and why didn't he say anything sooner?

But the only thing that comes out of my mouth is, "Uh. Yeah."

Austin takes that as an invitation, and maybe it is. Once again, his mouth crashes down on mine. He grabs hold of my clothes, and the bar that runs around the perimeter of the elevator makes me arch my hips forward.

"Zed," he says softly, using the nickname I told him I hated when we were still kids but he somehow never gave up on.

"Uh-huh?"

"I really wasn't flirting with Daniel."

Are we back to that again? I'm already over that whole thing. Have been for a while. Seems like the least of my worries at this point.

"No problem," I say. Why are we talking about that French assbag anyway? There are far more important matters immediately at hand.

But Austin's intent on explaining himself.

"I haven't flirted with anyone in months. Not since I realized I wanted you. Like, I'm totally, deeply, completely into you."

The elevator comes to a stop and the doors open on a soft *whoosh*. We don't move. Truthfully, I'm afraid to do anything because I'm so close to getting even the barest of answers and I don't want to break the spell like I did when I said his name. A few seconds later the doors close again, though the elevator stays on our floor.

"You what?" I ask.

The elevator goes so dead silent I can practically hear both our heartbeats. Or maybe it's that mine is so loud there's no room for anything else in my ears.

The elevator starts descending again. Shit.

Austin licks his lips, but when he exhales, his whole body relaxes, like he's come to a decision.

"I want you, Zed. Like, a lot. All the time. When we're training. Sleeping. Being with you . . . like, getting to touch you. Maybe even fuck someday . . . that's pretty much all I want."

He what?

"Are you screwing with me?" I try to crack a smile, but it fades just as quickly when his expression stays serious. Little spots of colour rise up on his cheeks. He's waiting for me to respond, and despite my surprise, I'm certain my answer is about to make some big decisions between us. So what do I say? Even if I were going to answer that I was flattered but maybe we should talk about it later when we haven't had anything to drink and everyone was calmer, I would never want to hurt Austin.

Only, I do want him. How could I not be attracted to him too? If he were a stranger, with his good looks and athletic build, I would want him the second I saw him. And since he knows me better than anyone else and still puts up with my ass . . .

"Hey," I say, snagging one of his beltloops. "Hey. It's okay. Let's go upstairs. Together."

The elevator doors slide open, once again revealing the lobby beyond. Before Austin can do another kiss-and-run, a group of women step on, forcing him back so he's standing beside me. The doors slide shut. They all have their backs to us, chatting about their trip here and who wants to stay up late watching Netflix. Austin is standing shoulder to shoulder with me. He looks like he's not breathing again. I scoot an inch closer to him, then let my hand fall, bumping against his knuckles once, twice, until finally I feel one of his fingers tangle with mine, then another. I grab hold of him, clasping his hand like a lifeline.

The women get off on the floor before ours and even when we're alone again, we don't speak. My heart is racing. Because of what he's said, and what's about to happen. It's *Austin*. I'm never going to want to only have sex with him and not talk about it again. Are we even having sex? He said he wanted to someday. Did he mean now? Maybe he only wants to cuddle until we get a few more things figured out? Maybe I'm overthinking everything for no reason.

We walk down the hall silently, still with our hands joined. There's no one around and my heart is in my throat. When I swipe my key card over the lock, my hands shake. I walk through the door, but Austin stays where he is, looking absolutely terrified.

"If we're doing this," I say, trying to sound more confident than I feel. "I can't take my clothes off with the door open. Someone might see."

That gets him moving. He stumbles over the threshold like I've finally said the magic words that will bring this Austin-shaped doll to life. The second the door closes behind him, he's on me again. It's like he only has two modes: terrified and hungry. Before I can say anything else, his hands are pulling at my clothes. When he can't get them off fast enough, he starts tugging at his own too, stripping the flannel and the clingy black base layer beneath in one go.

"Can we fuck tonight?" he asks, so apparently we really are going from zero to a hundred. Though that's hardly surprising. Austin and I have always been at our best when we're going as fast as possible, just on this side of losing control. Still, I can't stop the little zing of nerves in my belly when he takes my hands and asks, "Do you want to?"

Oh, I definitely want to. My hands and eyes rove over his naked chest. The flat stomach. Broad shoulders. The light brown hair that swirls over his pecs and down lower, disappearing beneath the waistband of his boxers. Who wouldn't want to fuck Austin Grimm, especially when he looks at them the way he's looking at me now?

I kiss him. Maybe for the first time. He's been the one out in front all night, but I'm finally starting to catch up. My tongue finds his and he moans with so much relief I can feel it all the way to my toes. This time, when he tugs at my shirt, I lift my arms over my head to help him. We tumble onto the bed and I cover his body with mine while also shimmying out of my pants. His skin has warmed up quickly and his strong hands cup my ass as he rocks against me.

"This isn't because of the beer, right?" I ask as I kiss his throat. "You're not going to sober up in a few hours and realize this was all a mistake?"

He bites my lower lip and the sting makes me hiss.

"The run up the hill cleared me right up," he says. "I know exactly what I'm doing."

He definitely does, wrapping a strong thigh over my hip to roll us so I'm on my back. Then he scoots down the mattress, until he's sprawled between my thighs. The outline of my cock is pretty evident in the tight fit of my briefs. Austin gives me a quick look, pale eyes twinkling, before he runs his tongue over the material, making my dick jump as it tries to escape the elastic.

"Holy shit," I say, arching up.

"Hold on," he says, peeling my underwear down. "I'm just getting started."

HE WORKS QUICK, I'll give him that. He's got a hand between us, stroking my cock. It's surprisingly gentle. I push my hips up, urging him on.

"Is that all you got?"

We haven't even turned the lights out and his smile is bright as he keeps working slowly.

"Trash talk and dirty talk are different things. You know that, right?"

"Not with me they aren't," I say, waggling my eyebrows. Now that we're on firmer emotional ground, I'm ready to play.

He laughs. "Whatever you say, Zed."

I flinch internally at the nickname. I got over my dislike for it years ago. But right now, it reminds me that once upon a time we were boys lying awake in our shared room the night before a junior race and Austin asked, "What do you think it's like to kiss a girl?" and my answer was "I've only ever thought about kissing boys."

We aren't those boys anymore.

"Call me something else," I say. "Only for tonight."

He looks up from where he was about to put my dick in his

mouth. My timing is terrible, but I need some ground rules to stay comfortable.

"Bear," he says with a smile, then he flicks his tongue over my slit, making me groan, more from the sensation than the name. He's called me Bear before—short for my last name, Berard—but it's never stuck the way Zed did. For tonight, it'll do.

He sucks me down, his mouth hot and slick. My dick in Austin's mouth is not where I thought my night was going as I picked snow out of my ears after my fall in the final, but we'll see who the winner is tonight.

I'm so wound up from everything, it only takes a minute or two before my balls tingle and draw up, getting ready to shoot like a skier in the starting gate.

"Stop," I say, putting a hand on the back of Austin's head. It can't be over yet. I pull out of his mouth, and a trail of saliva spills over his chin. When he goes to wipe it away, I sit up and catch his mouth with mine. It's messy. Sloppy. The trail becomes a smear, and I swipe my tongue over it. Austin whines. Slowly, I climb up the mattress until I'm leaning against the headboard. Austin follows, crawling like a predator, which only turns me on more. He straddles my hips, and his cock, long and curving slightly upward, bobs in invitation. I've seen it before, of course. We gave up on being shy about nudity pretty quickly as our winters on the race circuit got bigger and busier. Shared rooms and tight race schedules don't leave much space for modesty. But his dick has never been this close and begging for me. I eye him for a second, thinking about sucking him off now until he comes. He clearly wants it, and I'd find it very satisfying. Coming first isn't always a winning tactic, after all.

"Bear," he says softly, bumping the smooth head of his dick against my lips. I open for him. He's leaking already as he slides over my tongue. He tastes salty and the musk of his groin fills my nose. He's everywhere. All around me. I don't even have to do anything. Just hold still and keep my tongue flat as he pumps closer and closer until he finally hits the back of my throat and I gag.

"Sorry. Sorry." In a second, Austin slips free of my mouth, bending down to kiss me like he still wants to make it all better. His concern makes me laugh.

"I should probably admit that all the times we talked about blow jobs and how awesome I am at them, particularly when it comes to receiving, I was maybe exaggerating," I say. It didn't seem important at the time. Who hasn't talked up their bedroom prowess when hanging out with the guys? I didn't think it would ever become relevant to real life, or that I'd have to prove my supposedly legendary lack of a gag reflex to my best friend.

But Austin settles back on his heels, kissing me some more. It's nice. A little weird. He's so familiar and this is all so new. I run a finger over his collarbone, then past the freckles on his shoulder that I've seen a thousand times on a thousand summer days. A thousand afternoons at the gym. I kiss them, then work my way down his biceps and to the crease of his elbow, which makes him jerk, pulling his arm away.

"Ticklish?" I ask.

"No." But the curve of his mouth says otherwise. I bite my lower lip, thinking about my next move. He watches me, and his nostrils flare when he finally realizes where my train of thought is headed. "Don't you dare."

Too late. I grab him, flipping him over as I run my fingers over his sides, under his armpits and into that same sensitive spot at his elbow. He's always been ticklish, but it's not something I really took advantage of after middle school. Tonight, though . . .

"Stop," he says, squirming and laughing as he tries to get away.

"You sure?" I ask. I add my mouth back into the equation, kissing between his nipples while my fingers keep up their exploration.

"Yes. No. Oh god, Bear."

The name feels good. Right. Zed is a friend. A teammate. Bear is someone else. Someone more.

We still, breathing hard as we lie face to face. Austin arranges his expression into something I haven't seen before.

"This is enough," he says, brushing slow circles over my thigh. It's not tickling, exactly. More like a desire to stay connected. "If this is all we do tonight, I'm okay with that."

Unfinished blow jobs and tickle fights? I can do way better than that.

"And if I were someone else?" I ask. "If you'd come back here with someone from the bar? What would you do then?"

His fingers still. I don't push. We're not great at doing things slowly, but if that's what he wants tonight, I will do my best to go along with it. Might jerk off in the bathroom later, but I'll behave.

Still, I nearly weep with relief as Austin clears his throat before he says, "I'd get whoever it was to fuck me. Maybe more than once."

I nod, my body getting hot all over again at the idea of Austin riding my dick. Of the sounds he'll make and the sensation of him sliding around me.

"So we'll do that."

He blinks a few times, mouth falling slightly open.

"We don't have to."

But I want to. So much, in fact. Now that he's lying here, splayed out and willing, it seems impossible we've never done this before. He's so beautiful. Toned muscles undulate under his skin. Also, there's a tattoo of an orange cat with laser beams for eyes splayed out over one hip. He got it for his eighteenth birthday and I gave him so much shit for it, but now I can't help the way my mouth curls up at the corner as I study it. A tiny helpless city smoulders beneath the cat's attack and a helicopter circles overhead. Absurd chaos, like Austin himself.

Leaving him on the bed is torture, but I need reinforcements. I dig through the kit on the bathroom sink until I find what I'm looking for. When I get back, Austin's taken my spot on the headboard, lazily stroking himself as he watches me approach.

I hold up the condom between two fingers.

"I'm on PrEP, and I know you are too, but I'm not doing this without some backup."

His mouth quirks up. We tell each other everything. If there was even a fraction of a chance Austin had any kind of STI, he'd have said so. But I've got rules, and best friend or not, some rules can't be broken.

Our gazes lock for a moment. Austin licks his lips and swallows hard, before he gets up on his knees, presenting his ass and giving it a saucy wiggle in my direction.

"Is this okay?" he asks, sounding like a child eager to please. But there's nothing childish about him. Not the muscles or the tattoo or the thick penis that hangs between his legs. He's all man and he's in my bed.

Time to get what we came here for.

The small bottle of lube makes an embarrassing spattering sound as I squeeze it over his hole. Austin giggles.

"Excuse you," he says. His laughter makes his ass shake and the lube dribbles over his taint and balls. I bite my lip to keep from laughing too. This is supposed to be a big deal. Serious.

I roll my eyes. "Don't tell me you still laugh at fart jokes. What are you? Eight?"

"Fart jokes are hilarious at every age. They're—" Whatever he was about to say next is cut off on a gasp as I slide a finger inside him. His groan crackles all the way to my balls. How have we never done this before? Why did we wait for breathless confessions? As I work him open, moving quickly to add a second finger, he presses his mouth into the mattress and tangles his fingers into his hair.

He's so responsive. Every touch, every thrust of my fingers has him moaning. I'd could say it's because I know him. Know what he likes. Or that I'm a master of the delicate art of anal exploration. The truth is, there's a strong chance he can feel the way my hand is shaking, even from inside his ass, and a little vibration is never bad. My heart still hammers so hard it's loud in my ears, and my throat is dry. When I push in a third finger, his whole body rolls with pleasure, before he takes over, fucking himself against my hand. "Jesus, Ze—Bear," he says, sounding breathy. "If you don't fuck me soon, I'll come like this."

I would be happy with that. Everything that's happened so far is even better than I could have imagined. But I told him we'd do it, and I want him to be happy too.

I smack his ass. I don't even know if it's something he likes, but hopefully the sting will distract him long enough for me to get the condom on. My fingers shake and slip as I fumble with the latex. These things are always such a pain. It takes me a second to slide it down.

When I swing my attention back to Austin, he's watching me over his shoulder. He's braced on his elbows and once again shakes his ass. This time, it glistens invitingly with lube. I line myself up, picturing the tight heat I could feel with my fingers and how good it's going to feel around my dick, even with the latex. It's enough I nearly come before I get inside, but finally I flex my hips, and we both groan as we cross a threshold I never thought we would. He flexes, squeezing me with the ring of muscle that has welcomed me in. It's perfect. My first thrusts are slow, getting a feel for him. His body is firm. Ready for competition.

"You okay?" I ask.

"Uh-huh," he says, voice husky and low like I rarely hear from him. His shoulders are bunched up and trembling with tension.

I know what he needs. Slowly I back out, until only the very tip of me is still inside him.

"Three," I say.

"What?" He tenses even more.

"Two."

Austin huffs. "You can't be serious."

I don't give him a one. Instead, I slam in so hard the headboard bumps against the wall. Then I do it again. Austin pushes against me, grinding his hips as he backs his ass up against my pelvis.

"You like that?" I ask, not waiting for an answer before I continue. He's so hot and receptive underneath me. Everything I throw at him, he takes, opening his body and bracing himself on strong arms to withstand me no matter how rough I get. I tangle my hand in his long hair, forcing his head up, and he laughs but never loses his balance.

"Knew you'd be like this," he says. "I always knew. You can't back down from a—"

I kiss him. I don't need to hear his taunts. Just the way his body answers mine is enough. Whatever he wants from now until forever, I'm going to give it to him. It's embarrassing we didn't do this sooner, but maybe it's for the best. We got to work out our embarrassing teenage fumbling with other partners, so now we're ready for each other.

I lift him up so we're both on our knees. Austin takes over, slamming himself down on my cock over and over until he shudders, his body twisting and bucking. His ass tightens around my dick and he stills, breathing hard.

"You gonna come?" I ask, speaking into his ear as our bodies move in a perfect rhythm.

"Are you?" The question is a challenge. A dare. Winners really don't come first. Not always. Not tonight.

My fingers are still sticky with lube, and I spit in my palm, trying to create enough slickness that I can jack him off easily while I pump into his ass.

"Smart boy," he says, panting as I start to stroke.

"Not a boy. I'm older than you are," I say. The difference in our ages is only a couple weeks, but I'm not giving him any more ground tonight. When I tug at his earlobe with my teeth, he hisses, and his cock jumps in my hand. Good to know. At least in this position, I have more control over the rhythm of our fucking. Gravity holds him down, and my arm around his hips keeps him from rising up too high. I use my free hand to clasp around his throat, once again tipping his head back. He arches against me, cock leaking. I growl in his ear as I run my thumb through the slick at the top of his dick, smoothing it over the rounded head. He shudders, his muscles going tense. My own body is fighting me too. For release. For victory. I can't let him win. Not for a second time in one day.

"Come on," I let go of his cock long enough to pin his hips down against me while I flex. My teeth rake over his skin. The thick cords of his neck, the firm dome of his shoulder. He's perfection and now he's mine.

When I find his cock again, he whines. My hips pump upwards in a steady rhythm, and I slip a finger inside his mouth, tugging at the corner so he has to turn. Our kiss is messy. I stroke the tip of his dick, rubbing more fluid over the slit. He grits his teeth, trying to pull back from my kiss, and I bite down on his lip, refusing to let him go.

His cry is broken as he arches again, going taut against me. Semen slides over my hand and he pulses around my cock as he loses the fight, coming in sharp breaths and twitching muscles. As he sags, I push him down so he's back the way he was when we started. Face in the pillows, ass in the air. His sides heave as he tries to catch his breath and I watch, taking in the sight of what I've won. Not that he wasn't willing to let me have it.

It only takes two more thrusts before my balls draw up again. I pull out of him, yanking the condom off in time to shoot all over his glistening skin. My thighs shake like I'm at the end of a race, and I don't even need to touch myself to keep the orgasm going. My dick jerks and spurts and Austin collapses beneath me, spreading out over the bed in a jumble of limbs and quivering muscles.

Finally, when my body has ridden itself out, I slump back, sitting at the edge of the bed. My spunk shimmers on his skin and he makes no move to wipe it off or clean himself up. I can't help the warm satisfaction that bubbles over me at the sight. He might have started this, but I finished him.

Finally, Austin pushes up, chuckling softly. He walks naked through to the bathroom. I find my underwear and slide it back on, making sure to arrange myself casually when he returns.

Austin flops down on the mattress beside me, smiling a happy smile as he hums softly.

"That was good," I say, leaning back against the headboard. "We should do it again sometime."

He reaches up, pulling on my neck until I bend down to kiss him. His lips are still rough and hungry, and my spent dick twitches with interest.

"You think we're done?" Austin pulls the sheet away from the bed and rolls towards me, slinging one heavy thigh over mine. He kisses my shoulder, then pinches one of my nipples.

"I think today was a long day," I say. In so many ways. I'm still horny as shit, but the idea of falling asleep wrapped around Austin sounds pretty much perfect right now.

Austin, however, appears to have other plans.

"There's never only one run, Bear," he says, one hand sliding between my legs. "That was only the qualifier."

I glance at him. His eyes are full of heat and challenge. Changing the rules. Fine. I can play along.

I can go all night.

CHAPTER
FIVE

TRAINING IS part of any competition, and by midnight it becomes clear that in addition to our days in the gym and on the hill, Austin has been training for this kind of night for a long time. He is relentless. His mouth, hands, and ass all want me. Anytime. Any way. At one point, on the verge of falling asleep, I wake up to the wet sucking sounds of an enthusiastic blow job and find him between my thighs, mouth on my erect cock when I was sure I had nothing left in me to give. He looks up to find me watching and winks. He's working his own cock with his hand and when I crook my finger, he grins without ever losing his rhythm, turning himself to straddle my face as his dick dangles invitingly against my lips.

He is insatiable.

Also, he's a talker. For someone who's been holding onto a secret the size of wanting to sleep with his best friend, now that the dam has burst, he can't seem to stop.

"Do you remember that night in California last year?" he asks, lying across my chest. We're both in that quiet post-orgasm haze where honesty comes out uninvited.

"You'll have to be more specific." We competed in California last year, but we also went to a clinic in the off-season near Tahoe.

Functional mobility and strength training. A lot of days of sweating and straining. Austin was clearly getting ready for tonight. Would have been nice if he'd given me the heads-up too.

"The night you took Jihoon back to our room," he says.

My cheeks sizzle. There had been a small contingent from South Korea at the clinic. They're not a country with a long history of success in snow sports but they've been making strides in the last few years. All the more reason for them to come to the clinics and training events, really. And it had mixed up the list of possible partners for some nighttime training of our own. Jihoon had been . . . yeah. That was a good night. The goggles were on the doorknob for a long time.

Then I remember it's not Jihoon I'm in bed with now, and reminiscing so fondly is probably some kind of rules violation. I clear my throat and say, "Uh-huh?"

Austin's eyes are closed, so hopefully he didn't notice my lapse in attention. He says, "The next day, when we were doing that workshop on visualization techniques, we were supposed to be thinking about ski trails and snow conditions. All I could think about was you. The sounds you'd make. The way it would feel if it were me with you instead of him. It freaked me out how much I wanted you."

A few nearly forgotten pieces click into place. Austin had been weird that whole weekend. A lot of badly hidden glances and facial expressions that didn't fit with what was going on around us. The idea that he'd been preoccupied with me and what it would be like for us to go to bed together is exciting in a way I don't expect. I groan as my dick perks up yet again, enticed by the image of his jealousy. Then I groan some more when I slide a thigh between Austin's and find he's hard too.

"Are we at least out of the qualifiers?" I ask. I have no idea what time it is or how long we've been at this. I only know I don't want it to stop. Ever.

He strokes me, bringing me to increasing hardness.

"I'd say we're definitely at the semis by now."

The hours tick by.

"I think I'm in love with you," he says, in the dark hours of the night. I'm so wrecked I don't even have the energy to respond, but he keeps talking anyway. "I promised myself I'd wait until after the Olympics before I said it. I know you have a plan for qualifying and this could be a huge distraction for you, but I don't want to wait anymore."

I shouldn't have done that. Not yet.

Does he have the date he planned to say he loved me penciled in on a calendar somewhere? Circled and decorated with hearts? Planning is more my thing. As is thinking through my feelings. My face goes hot and my ears ring as I consider his confession. Tonight has been amazing. Way more than a casual hookup with a stranger from a faraway place. But even in the protective cocoon of the smallest hours before dawn, I don't know that I'm ready to make the same admission.

Austin frames my face with his hands as he spreads his body on top of me. His kisses get softer. Gentler. Like once again he's trying to make everything better.

"It's okay if you don't say it back," he says, because of course he knows what I'm thinking. We know each other too well to hide secrets. Well . . . except for one big secret Austin's been keeping for a long time. How did I never notice? But he doesn't seem to be too worried, because he says, "I know you don't feel the same way. Not yet, anyway."

My mouth works on words I don't even understand. I do love him. He's been with me through everything. Seen things and experienced things no one else in the world would ever truly understand, no matter how many times my parents ask me how a training trip went, or how often coaches tell me what I'm working through is normal and to keep pushing.

But am I *in* love with him? It's not about avoiding distractions. It's about stepping over a line I've never crossed before. "Better off as friends" can be such a cop-out, but what if in this case it's true?

But also, what if it's not?

Instead of saying anything, I kiss him some more, and he doesn't protest my silence.

Later yet, I'm staring at the ceiling, watching the soft blink of the smoke detector overhead. We still haven't turned all the lights out, and Austin is illuminated by the small light on the nightstand next to him. He's got his back to me, one arm flung over his face to shield his eyes. I roll, thinking distantly I might reach over him and turn the light out, but when I press up against him, he makes a sleepy pleased sound.

"Missed me already?" he asks. He rocks his ass against my groin, bringing me back to life one more time. The room wheels like I'm drunk, even though the effects of our celebratory beers must have worn off hours ago. My fingers feel heavy, distant, like it's someone else touching him. He whines when I roll away, then laughs softly as I pull the last condom out of the pack, sliding it on with hands that shake for entirely different reasons than they did the first time. Then it was nerves. Adrenaline. Now it's exhaustion. I wanted to break Austin, but he is very close to breaking me.

When I slide into him this time, there's no resistance. He won't walk straight for days after this. Austin has to be sore, but his moan as I move in and out of him is only pleasure.

"Yes," he says, bringing one of my arms over to cradle against his chest. "Yes."

It's never been like this for me. Not with anyone. Austin must coat his skin in something addictive. They'll do a drug test and suspend me from competition and all I'll be able to say is that it wasn't some unmarked supplement or cold medication. It was Austin Grimm. I can't get enough of him.

Our orgasms are almost pathetic. No more rockets and lightning. Just a long exhale and a twitch for him, a grunt from me and we're done.

God, I hope we're done.

"You good?" he asks, as I slip the condom off and bunch it up in a shitty single-ply hotel tissue. The idea of getting up and walking to the trash can feels like doing an uphill run in a weighted vest. I drop it on the nightstand.

"Of course. Why wouldn't I be?" I run a hand over his hip, brushing my fingers over the laser cat.

"I didn't mean to spring this on you," he says.

I snort and wrap him up with rubbery arms. "Are you still apologizing? You may have had the realization before I did, but a few more nights like this, and you won't be able to get rid of me." I kiss the top of his head, enjoying the absolute sense of rightness that comes with the feeling of Austin smelling like sex and sweat in my arms. He got off the start line before I did, but I've been giving chase all night and I'm pretty close to catching up. He won't have to worry about being jealous of me and someone else ever again. There won't be anyone else.

Provided I don't die of exhaustion first. Maybe tonight hasn't been some epic love confession. Maybe this is Austin's idea of revenge. Can't fuck around if I'm too tired to live.

I yawn. My eyelids feel like lead weights. "What time is it?"

Austin pulls his watch off the nightstand, squinting at the face. It's an old analogue watch that was given to him when his grandfather died back while we were in high school. He says it's his lucky charm.

"It's five thirty. Shit."

"What?" Unless he's about to tell me the world is ending at sunrise, whatever he's worried about can wait until I've had some sleep.

"The shoot."

My drowsiness makes it hard to follow what he's saying.

"What shoot?"

He shakes me. The motion is urgent. I have a sinking feeling sleep is about to escape me for a little longer.

"The Apex shoot."

My eyes fly open.

"Now?"

"We have to be downstairs at six." He looks at me, face stricken.

Ugh. Apex is one of the team's major sponsors. They do high-performance winter apparel, and next year they're producing the suits we'll be wearing for competition, including at the Olympics. With this being the last race of this season, they scheduled a photoshoot for the day after, since the whole team would be available. The pictures are going to be used for promotional campaigns across Canada next winter in the run up to the Games. The hassle of doing it already seemed like a pain last night before we went out for karaoke. Now, though? How dare they interrupt my sleep? I'd even go for round nine—or is it fourteen?—with Austin instead of dragging myself from this bed so I can pretend to be excited about wearing a designer ski suit I could never afford on my own.

But Austin's already up, running around, scrambling for his clothes.

"I completely forgot about it. I can't believe I forgot."

I can. Man had other priorities and I respect that. I roll onto my back, groaning. This can't be how tonight ends.

"What if we didn't show up?"

Austin's halfway into his underwear but gets his foot stuck, sending him reeling backward until he flops back down on his bed, the one we haven't touched all night.

"Forget it," I say, pulling the blankets up around my ears. "I'm not going."

"Then Tara would make us both sorry." He rests his chin on his palm as he looks up at me, arching an eyebrow. I groan again. He's not wrong. Behind her back, a lot of the racers refer to Tara the Terror. She's our sponsorship liaison. We all know sponsors are the only reason we're able to compete at this level. Their money funds our training and, for a lot of us, even things like housing. Without companies like Apex, most of us would need part-time jobs at a minimum, which would take up time we don't have if we want to keep training and competing. We know this because Tara reminds us of it every time someone gets mopey about chatting up potential sponsors or doing an event with them when we'd rather be skiing. She will not take no for an answer under any circumstances short of catastrophic injury or death.

"Fine." I push him off me. "I'm taking a shower. Can't show up stinking like you. Everyone will know what we've been up to."

Not that the shower will help much. I'm covered in hickeys. Austin's a mouthy bastard. I groan for entirely new reasons as I examine myself in the mirror while the water heats up. He managed not to mark up my neck or face too badly, but my shoulders, arms and chest are a minefield of bruises. We're going to have to have a talk about that.

But first, photoshoot. Hickey lectures can wait.

CHAPTER
SIX

I'M TWENTY MINUTES LATE. Austin is dressed by the time I'm out of the shower. I tell him not to wait. Once I'm clean, I get dressed, then somehow find myself slumped forward on the edge of the bed where I've fallen asleep while trying to put my socks on. I say a little prayer that Tara's feeling merciful this morning as I quickly down two cups of coffee from the hotel room's tiny coffee maker.

When the elevator doors slide open, it's like every person in the lobby turns to stare at me. Everyone's there. Matthieu. Kage. The women's team is milling around too. I think about going back upstairs until I spot Austin, sitting in a tall folding chair, and I square my shoulders. He has to feel as much like shit as I do. I can't leave him hanging.

Unfortunately, before I can go check in with him, Tara the Terror spots me and rushes across the lobby to intercept.

"You're late. I specifically said six o'clock, not six thirty," she says, tugging on my sleeve.

"It's not six thirty. It's only—" I glance at my phone and, yeah. Six twenty-four. I could argue if I want to, but the flash in her eyes says I'm playing with fire if I do.

She guides me to a tall chair like Austin's and calls for makeup.

"Makeup? What for?" I ask. No one said anything about makeup. Who's going to see my face once I'm in full ski gear?

Tara snorts, eyeing me closely. "Trust me. You look like you didn't sleep a wink last night. Didn't I tell you not to go out and get wasted? And what the hell happened to your face?"

After so many hours of Austin slowly melting my brain and changing me from the inside out, I'd forgotten about the bruise where Daniel punched me until I looked at myself in the bathroom mirror. Even without the hickeys, my face should be enough to disqualify me from today's events, but Tara's not accepting anything less than full team participation.

Also, despite the early hour, she looks perfect. Reddish-blond hair swept up in a messy bun, but I know the strands that tumble free around her face were specifically chosen for the role. Her makeup is flawless. Lips a glossy pink. Eyeliner fiercely black and delicately arched. Beside her, I probably do look like roadkill.

Grumbling, I slump into the seat. At least I get to sit next to Austin. A stylist is doing something with his hair, making it look windblown, which I guess is better than the last time I saw it, when it was sticking out at odd ends and basically screaming "freshly and excessively fucked." I give him a quick smile and go to ask if he feels as shitty as I do, then hesitate. We didn't talk about this. Alone in the hotel room, being together felt real. Like something that was meant to be and will last for a long time. But out here, with so many of the people we see every day, I don't know how we're supposed to behave. Not that I'm afraid of judgment. It's ski cross, not conservative politics. No one cares that we're queer, and there are probably even a few people who are about to cash in on some friendly wagers on whether or not Austin and I are a couple. But we didn't exactly have time to agree on how and when we go public.

The problem is solved when a pushy makeup artist arrives, grabbing my chin and *tsk*ing as though my face has craters like the moon and not just some dark circles and a puffy cheek. At one point, the artist pulls aside the collar of my shirt and the look he gives me says he thinks the marks on my skin might be contagious. I tell him not to worry, that I'll keep my jacket zipped up and he sniffs softly before he continues working on my face. By the time I'm done, Austin's hair has achieved maximum windage and he's waiting with the others by the hotel's front door.

"Rough night?" Kage asks as I approach. "We didn't see you two leave the bar."

I glance at Austin, who quirks his mouth up in a careless grin.

"We wanted to make sure we were well rested for the shoot today," he says.

Fair enough. We can save the big announcements for later.

We're all loaded into vans and driven around to the far side of the mountain. The sun is barely over the horizon and will hit this side of the hill first. The Apex team and their photographers are waiting for us, armed with a fleet of snowmobiles to take us up the trail and tubs of outerwear for us to wear during the shoot. It's so early, the chairlifts aren't even running yet, but one of the brand reps tells us they've booked a whole trail for our use, so even once the day's skiers arrive, we won't be bothered.

I feel like absolute shit. The coffee sits in the bottom of my stomach like battery acid. The Apex people haven't exactly provided a full catering spread, since a hot breakfast doesn't travel well up the side of a snow-covered mountain, but there's a table set up with muffins and protein bars. I try a muffin, but the inside of my mouth is so dry it basically sticks in my throat like glue. Also, my whole body hurts. Spending a weekend competing at an international ski cross event, followed by nonstop sex with your best friend is a physically demanding undertaking. My knees and hips ache, my thighs shake when I do a few test turns, there's even a weird kink in the middle of my back that pulls every time I turn my head to the right.

"You okay?" Austin asks as we wait for our turn at the shoot.

"Are you?" I ask.

He smiles softly to himself. "My ass hurts."

Is that all? I didn't do my job right if it is.

"How long is this thing supposed to go for?" I ask.

"Tara said we'd be done by noon."

I groan. Turns out photoshoots aren't fast moving things, especially not when there's a whole team to shoot and the clothing company has brought multiple sets of gear for everyone to wear. We don't even get to do a proper run. Just five or six turns until we're past the camera, then the snowmobiles tow us back up to the starting point so we can do it again while the photographer shouts at us to look at the camera or not look at the camera, to smile or not smile. Sometimes we go alone and other times in pairs. On and on.

I have a headache.

"Kill me now," I say as the snowmobile deposits me back at the top of the run so I can change into my third coat of the day. My legs are shaking, my arms are throbbing from holding onto the tow line as I get pulled back up the hill, and even if I blink, there's two of everything unless it's right in front of me.

Like Austin. He slides into my field of view, coming to a sharp stop as he smiles at me with flushed cheeks.

"Isn't this fun?" he asks.

"Sleep would be fun." I yawn. "Are we almost done?"

"Soon. And then . . ." His smile gets wider. Mischievous.

My throat goes dry. "And then?"

He waggles his eyebrows, leaning in close so no one else could hear. "I'm going to make you scream my name until you think it's your own."

I have to brace on my poles to keep from collapsing entirely.

"You're a menace," I say. "You can't say things like that."

He bites the tip of his tongue. "Why not? You think I can't?"

I close my eyes and focus on steadying my breath. Thank god for the layers of outerwear I've got on, which at least hide my swelling cock from anyone's notice.

Also, I have no doubt that Austin can and most likely will

succeed on his mission, but I need sleep. We've all been booked for one extra day on the resort for today's shoot, but first thing tomorrow I have to drive back to Quebec City, where the team has its training facility. The drive is four hours on mostly winding regional roads and no interstates. I need rest.

I must say that last part out loud, because Austin shakes his head, giving me the same weary look the makeup artist did earlier.

"I expected more from you, Zed," he says, poking at my chest.

I swat him away. "Just a couple hours. A cat nap. You want me performing at my best, don't you?"

His face is impossibly close to mine. As soon as anyone notices, the cat's out of the bag. There's no way we can hide what we're about to do, not with the way Austin's lips are millimetres from mine.

"Grimm! Berard! Enough with the staring contest," Tara yells, glaring at us. She's gripping the tablet that houses her master schedule of pairings and pictures to be taken. "Get changed and get ready for your last shoot."

I could cry with relief. We shed our coats and pants, putting on the new ones given to us.

When it's our turn, Tara says, "Okay. When you're done, keep going down to the base. The van will drive you back to the resort. The concept for these shots is a race. You think you two dorks can manage that?"

Austin and I glance at each other, and suddenly all my exhaustion evaporates. If there's one thing we can do even when we're beyond exhausted, it's race. We've been trying to conclusively prove who can get from the top of the mountain to the bottom fastest for thirteen years. No amount of fatigue can stop us. Not even when mixed with extreme horniness and the revelation my best friend is in love with me and I'm not at all freaked out about it.

When we get the signal, Austin and I push off. We hold back for the first few turns, waiting until we're beyond the camera team, then we blow past the snowmobiles and Austin whistles. The sound is loud and sharp and it's not a horn in a starting gate but it's close enough. I lean into my boots, bending my knees. My muscles protest, but tough shit. It's a race to the base and then to my bed. No way I'm coming last on this one.

The wind picks up as we fly down the trail. It's not especially steep. Less pitch than the run we raced on yesterday. But it's enough to pick up some speed, particularly in the places where the tall trees at the edges of the trail have kept the sun off the snow and it's still packed hard. The trail is also narrower than a standard ski cross course, so even though there are half as many competitors, we're still going to have to keep together if we want the fastest line. There are even some nice curves to keep it interesting.

"On your left," Austin calls from behind my shoulder. The scrape of his skis is incredibly close.

"Fuck's sake. This is a race, not a run down a lazy river. I know you're—" But I don't get to finish before he slides past me, whooping as he goes by. His posture is relaxed, hands held low, but ready to brace when the next turn comes. The trail gets narrower, the trees pressing in closer.

We come over a rise and he catches some air, and I follow half a second behind him. The world is silent, no scraping edges, no snow being thrown to the sides as we pass. Just the wind in my ears and, only slightly ahead of me, Austin's heavy breathing, before we come down in fast sequence on the snow. *Whap, whap.* My knees and hips ache with the impact, still protesting all their overnight mistreatment. When we get to the bottom—no, when *I* get to the bottom—and back to my room, I'm going to take the longest soak in the hot tub. Ideally with Austin, his ass firmly planted on my dick as I—

I shake my head, pushing the thought away. No distractions. At this level of competition, it's not really about who's a better technical skier. It's about who has the stronger focus and mindset. Letting your mind wander is a one-way ticket to fourth place.

There's another curve in the trail coming up ahead. It's even narrower than the ones we've been through. It's the perfect place to take advantage and claim the lead. There's a dip on the low side that should leave me a little room to ski by, and if I push Austin up as I go, he'll have no choice but to swing toward the trail edge, losing ground and time.

He must see it too. I'm only a couple inches behind his shoulder, and his posture tenses, searching for milliseconds of speed that will keep him in front. I let off on my edges as we head for the turn. We're really flying now. My body screams over every bump and jostle, but if I stay focused on the point ahead, where the turn lets out into a broad expanse that will lead to the base, he'll have no chance of catching me.

We both lean into the turn. We're so close I have to be careful where I put my uphill hand so I don't hit his. I hit another snag where snow gives way to slick ice, and I push him higher than I mean to. Any farther up and I'll be the one losing speed too. Hopefully he sees my grin as I blow past him, dropping my shoulder into the final curve and—

"Fuck! Bear!"

For a second I think he means there's a bear. It's not unheard of on mountains for skiers to have wildlife encounters. Then I remind myself we're in New England. This isn't exactly grizzly country. Still, I turn my head uphill, checking to make sure I'm not being pursued by anything furry and angry.

In fact, I'm not being pursued by anything. Or anyone.

"Austin?" Involuntarily, I slow. I don't want to stop, in case he's playing some kind of trick and he's about to pop out of the trees farther down the trail where I'll have no hope of catching him if I'm not already moving.

But he doesn't come out of the trees. Doesn't come out of anywhere.

Where the hell did he go?

"AUSTIN? AUSTIN!" I call his name, then hold my breath waiting for his answer. The mountain is silent, aside from the sound of wind in the trees and a faraway crow who may also be calling for a friend.

"Grimm!"

Still nothing.

It's fine. He's fine. He's an experienced skier. One of the best in the world. He might have wiped out on that last corner, but he's okay. Just picking snow out of his ears like I did yesterday. In a second, he'll pop back into view and shout he's okay, because that's what we always do.

The crow calls again, echoing over the empty trail.

I put my fingers to my lips, blasting out a single whistle. Even if he can't hear my voice, he'll be able to hear that and reply. We've done it before, if we ever get separated and wind up taking different trails to the bottom.

But five, ten, fifteen seconds later there's still no answer and my heart goes cold.

"Austin!" I struggle to get my skis off, banging at the bindings until I finally pop free. Running up in the direction of the turn where I last saw Austin is tough going. Ski boots aren't exactly made for trail running. The rigid plastic creaks and the small square toe piece digs into the snow with a rhythmic *chk chk*. I'm breathing hard as I approach the turn, and my chest squeezes painfully at the sight of two parallel lines that disappear over the edge of the trail. Austin's ski tracks. He must have caught some air, because they don't continue down the slope. I call for him again, straining for any sound. There's a spot in the snow farther down that looks like it's been disturbed, but it might be a person falling, or snow that's fallen from the branches of the trees.

"Austin!"

Finally, an answer comes. Sort of an answer. It's not an animal, but it's barely human. No words, only a long low moan from somewhere beyond the divot in the snow. I throw myself down the slope, swinging my arms to stay balanced and not smash into a tree.

"Grimm!"

I find a pole. A ski, then another one. They're strewn in the snow like massive breadcrumbs, marking the trail—if it can be called a trail—Austin took. Shit, he must have been really moving. Of course he was, since he was trying to keep up with me.

Also, the snow is thin down here. Early spring melt has left the ground uneven, with humps of snow against tree trunks, and muddy brown paths between where water has started to flow. Along with stumps and branches, jagged rocks break through the surface, and the sight of them in line with the path of Austin's discarded equipment makes my heart stop.

What if he really is hurt?

I nearly fall myself, plastic boots skidding in the mud. I have to grab hold of a tree to stay upright.

That's when I see him.

Austin is lying in the snow, arms and legs splayed out at odd angles. He must have fallen this whole way and the only thing that stopped him is the large rock he's rolled up against. I slide to a halt next to him, falling to my knees.

"Austin? Hey. Hey! Can you hear me?" I ask, hands shaking as

I try to pull off my gloves. He moans, the sound broken and rough, then flails like he can't get all his body parts to work at the same time.

"Shh. Shh. It's okay. Don't move." All I can think of is words like "spinal cord" and "head injury."

But he either doesn't hear me or doesn't care, because he flops backward onto the snow. It's an uncoordinated movement, and his face is a mess of blood as I catch his head in my lap.

Holy shit. Holy shit!

"Austin? Can you hear me?" I don't want to touch him, but also I do. His goggles are shattered, and there's a terrifying spiderweb of cracks in the front of his helmet. He's breathing funny, like he can't get the air all the way down to his lungs. Panic makes my own breathing ragged as I try to think what to do. Something from a distant first aid course. Airways, breathing . . . shit, those are the same things, aren't they . . . what was the C part of the acronym?

I'm in over my head.

"Shh. Shh. It's okay. You're okay. You're going to be okay." The words are a stream of babble that don't really mean anything. I look back up the slope I've come down. I can see the edge of the trail, but nothing else.

The phone. They have 9-1-1 here, right? I fumble for the pockets in my coat before I remember this isn't mine. My phone is in the pocket of my actual coat, which I left at the base before they sent us up on the snowmobiles. The realization is like a punch to the gut and for a minute I can barely breathe.

When I finally manage a decent inhale again, I scream.

"Help! Help!" My voice echoes through the trees. Fear grips my throat, strangling my calls. We need more than help. We need a rescue. Austin is in bad shape. He still hasn't spoken, but his left leg is bent in a sickening position, and there's something wrong with his arm, because he keeps trying to flex his hand like he wants to lift it off the snow, then lets it fall to the ground again. Dislocated, maybe. I've seen it before. You hang around skiers going fast downhill long enough, you've seen most injuries. Sprained wrists, dislocated shoulders. Broken noses, ribs and collarbones, torn knees.

But I've never seen them all at once.

Austin makes a wet choking sound. Spinal injury be damned. Who cares if he can't walk later if he asphyxiates on his own blood now? I roll him gently on his side and he coughs up a mouthful of blood onto the gritty snow.

"Help!" I call again. There have to be more people coming down. If Tara said we could go, she'll be telling others the same. I can't see skiers on the trail, but one of them should hear me. While I keep calling, I pull my coat off, slipping it behind Austin's back to keep him from rolling away. He makes a choked sobbing sound when I move him.

"I know. I know," I murmur. "They're coming. Just hold tight. Someone's going to hear us and bring help." I pull my helmet off and add it to the pile, squeezing it between the coat and the rock that stopped Austin's headlong fall into the brush. There's a smear of red on the stone and I look away, trying not to think about what part of Austin's body left that behind.

"Bear," he says. The word is frighteningly weak. I brush some of the blond strands of his hair out of his face, tucking them behind one ear. The ends are coated in blood. Not that long ago, my fingers were tangled in that same hair, pulling it back so he could take my dick a little bit easier. How did we get from there to here?

"Bear?" he says again, and my heart stops, because I realize his warning before had nothing to do with a random bear on the side of the trail. He was saying my name. The stupid nickname that was only between us in the dark hours of the night. He wasn't shouting a warning, he was calling for help. Calling for me.

"Yeah," I say, fingers and voice shaking equally hard as I brush at his hair some more. "Yeah. I'm here. Don't worry, the ski patrol is on their way."

Are they, though? No one even knows we're down here. It

feels like we sit in the snow forever. The cold and wet soak through my ass, because even waterproof cutting-technology pants can't stay waterproof forever when you're sitting in melting snow with a man's head in your lap as he struggles to breathe. The sound goes from wet to shallow. The blood that was initially flowing from his nose slows, but a trickle slides from the corner of his mouth, and he coughs again, whimpering softly at the end. The whole time, I replay those last seconds in my head over and over. The race. The trail. A tight corner. Nothing we haven't battled through before. So what was different this time?

Finally, the hiss of skis on snow comes from somewhere overhead. I suck in the biggest lungful of air I can and let out a scream loud enough to make the snow in the trees shake.

There's a pause, and I can't even hear the swish of the skier anymore. Tears threaten to spill over from my eyes. I can't leave him here. But if I don't go back up to the trail, no one will ever find us.

"Hello?"

I sag at the sound of someone's voice.

"Yes! Yes, we're down here! Help!"

A head appears at the edge of the trail, then another.

"Cedric?" It's Matthieu.

"Help! Austin needs help! Get the ski patrol."

There's some conversation between Matthieu and his companion, but only a few seconds later, Matthieu has his skis off and planted at the edge of the trail in the X shape that signals danger or an accident. He slides down the hill toward me, and I can only hope whoever was with him has called for help.

"Calice." Matthieu swears in French as he falls next to me. He's breathing hard from his run, but his cheeks are pale as he stares down at Austin's bloody face.

"He fell," I say, voice cracking now that someone knows we're here. "We were racing and he went over the side. I don't know. I didn't see, but he—" The words end on a sob. I can't say it. I don't even know the extent of his injuries. He hasn't spoken in minutes and his breathing is getting shallower and slower. I keep petting his hair like he's a puppy.

By the time the ski patrol arrives, following the same treacherous path down through the trees, Austin is completely still. I've got one hand inside the front of his coat because I need to feel the beat of his heart against my palm to convince myself he's not already dead. His body is so cold, even through the layers of insulation and microfibre meant to keep him warm. I find myself murmuring to him over and over to hang on, until the words don't even mean much in my head.

The ski patrol takes forever getting him back up onto the trail. In theory, they must be trained for this, but most of their job involves loading up weekenders who have sprained a thumb or broken a leg. One of them has a radio he uses to contact the base, using words like "air transport" and "catastrophic injury." They strap Austin onto the rigid sled that doubles as a back board. Another of the ski patrollers says something to me, but it takes a second to tear my eyes away off Austin's motionless form.

"What?" I ask.

"I said are you okay? Are you hurt anywhere?"

I don't know how much time has passed since the moment Austin vanished over the edge of the trail. Minutes, maybe. Hours, possibly. If someone said I'd been sitting by this bloody rock for days until help arrived, I'd believe them. Coming back to my body to check for injuries feels like it takes almost as long.

"I'm fine," I say, though I wobble as I push to stand and have to plant a hand on the rock to keep from toppling over. My foot is asleep inside my boot. Not much room to wiggle my toes or ankle to get the blood flowing again. But when I let go of the rock and lift my hand free, there's plenty of blood on my palm. Only it's not mine. Austin left it there.

Jesus Christ. How did this happen? It was a friendly race after what was a long morning and a longer night.

No one will quite meet my eyes when we reach the edge of the trees. The ski patrol is already double checking Austin is secure before one of them steps between the extended handles of the sled and heads down the mountain. The entire entourage of Apex snowmobiles and staff have appeared, along with Tara and other teammates. The snowmobiles bring the rest of us down, following the sled like a gruesome funeral procession. But he's not going to die. I say it to myself over and over. People don't die from skiing accidents. Except of course they do. Head injuries. Internal bleeding. Austin could very well have all of those.

The helicopter is already coming in for a landing in the resort parking lot. Onlookers have gathered to see what's going on and I say a silent thank you that at least, dressed in our Apex gear and not our national team jackets, we look like anyone else. Ski cross may not get a lot of media coverage, but this isn't the story we want to make.

"Can I go with him?" I ask, but I already know the answer. Not a lot of room in a helicopter. Austin's going to a hospital a few towns away. The local resort town only has a small clinic meant to deal with minor injuries and illnesses. I feel numb as Tara herds us all into the vans. A few people ask if I'm okay. A few others ask what happened. Matthieu sits himself between me and everyone else, and distantly I can hear him saying to give me some space. All I can think is that I should be with Austin.

And that this is all my fault.

I kept asking myself what was different that our race went so far off course, and the answer is *we* were. Distracted. Exhausted. We were up all night after racing all weekend. No one should have been doing more than a gentle snow plow under those circumstances.

"He's going to be okay," Matthieu says to me. I nod, trying to believe him.

It was a meaningless race. A pointless sprint like the thousands of ones we've challenged each other to over the years. Sometimes I win. Sometimes he does. We give each other a hard time. Maybe buy a round of drinks. No one ever goes to the hospital. All I had to do was give him enough room around that turn. Instead, I pushed too hard and—

"I'll call his family," Tara says as we get off the van. "They should know."

I hadn't even thought about his family. His parents, Donna and Patrick. They still live in Ottawa. They didn't come this weekend, even though it was one of the closest races this season because Patrick tweaked his back last week moving a couch. Austin's their youngest kid. His two older sisters, Mathilda and Nicki, both live in Toronto. They're all going to be so scared for him.

"Thanks," I say, though I don't know why. Because I was there? Because I'm his best friend? Would everyone still be so nice to me if they knew I'd basically pushed him off the side of the trail?

Once we enter the lobby, I'm left alone. I shuffle to the elevator, riding up in silence. But walking into the room is like slamming into a brick wall. The scattered sheets. The crumpled tissues on the night stand. The scent of sex and Austin that permeates the air.

Holy fuck, I'm going to fall over.

My breath is coming in short, sharp gasps as I stagger to the bed. I shake uncontrollably as I fall onto the mattress. My teeth chatter and my hands ball up into fists. What the fuck? I'm okay. I'm fine. What the hell is going on with me? It's Austin who's somewhere between here and the hospital. Maybe he's already there. Maybe he's already having surgery. He can't die, right? Skiing is all about falling. He'll get back up, right?

My stomach rolls and I barely make it to the bathroom before I throw up. Shock, some distant part of my brain says. Can I go into shock if I'm not the one who was hurt? My whole body aches as I stagger to my feet and rinse my mouth out at the sink.

I don't remember falling asleep. Don't even remember deciding to get into the bed or wrapping myself up in the blankets that smell like the two of us. Distantly, I think hear someone knocking on my hotel room door, but I can't find it in myself to get up and see who it is. When I wake up, Austin's old watch is wrapped in my fist, the plain face shining in light that filters out from the bathroom. Did I turn it on when I came in? Is it still on from my hasty shower this morning? From last night when we were so excited to undress each other and touch and fuck that we never even worried about the lights?

Doesn't matter. I can't stay here. Can't sit here waiting.

I shrug into clothes and hurry downstairs to find a cab.

Austin needs me.

THE DRIVE to the hospital takes more than a half hour and the cab driver grumbles the whole time about how far away from home I'm taking him. He's still getting paid; I don't know what the problem is. He practically squeals out of the parking lot once he drops me off in front of the hospital's main entrance.

I have a plan. It's not a great one. I'm not someone who likes to work on the fly. My success in racing has come from careful training and preparation. But if I've learned anything in the last day, it's that even on the most carefully traced course, you still have to be able to make adjustments as you go, and that's what I'm doing now.

I go in through the large sliding doors. The town is small enough that even the ER is fairly quiet. Tired-looking people sit in chairs in the waiting area. A scowling nurse sits behind a glassed-in desk. I keep up my heavy breathing as I walk in, and even manage to squeeze out a few tears as I approach.

"Can I help you?" she asks, fingers already poised over the keyboard, ready to take a record of whatever sniffle or injury has brought me to her ER.

I gasp, like I'm trying to stuff down a sob. It's not hard. All I can think is that somewhere in this building, Austin is hurt and alone. Sure, there are doctors and nurses, and they're invested in helping him, but there's no one here who knows him.

"I'm looking for my boyfriend," I say, leaning hard into my French-Canadian side so I sound like my grandfather and—most importantly—like someone unfamiliar.

She looks at me over her bright blue glasses. "Your boyfriend."

I nod, stifling another gasp-sob. She stares at me like there's no way she believes I'm anyone so important as a boyfriend. And am I? This time last night I was a trusted best friend being dragged out for karaoke. But the way my heart will not stop pounding in my ears and my chest feels very boyfriend-like indeed.

"Austin Grimm. They said he had an accident. Please. I drove all the way down from Quebec City. It took hours. They said he almost died. Please." I pull the watch from my pocket, holding it up to the glass. "It's a family heirloom. He never takes it off, but somehow he forgot it before he came down for the weekend. That's why he got hurt. He needs it back. Please, I need to know he's okay." With every word I let my voice drift a little higher and make the words wobble more. Her fingers tense up on the keyboard. Hopefully we're at the end of her shift and I'm one too many hysterical patients or family members she's had to deal with today.

"Visiting hours were over at six," she says.

I shake my head, turning my eyes to what I hope is a pleading look. "No. Listen. I've been in the car for hours. I'm the only family here. His parents can't come and his sisters live in a different province. I need to know he's okay." My voice cracks on the last part. That sentence is true. All I want tonight is to see him with my own eyes. If I know he's awake and alive, then I can ignore the accusations that keep swirling around in my head. The ones that say I'm responsible. The race was a bad idea. The trail was too narrow and I should have known that. We were too tired to stand up, much less have the reflexes needed to make it to the bottom of the run safely. If I can see him, I will put the questions to bed, even if I can't sleep myself. Maybe I'll give him a hard time about the lengths he's gone to in order to avoid a second round with me tonight. It was his suggestion after all. He could have told me he'd changed his mind.

The nurse gives me a weary stare, but finally she says, "He'll be in the ICU. Talk to the nurse up there. I'll let him know you're coming."

I get a little lost. Hospitals are like that. When I finally find the ICU, the nurse is already waiting for me in the hall. I puff up, getting ready to bring on my overwrought boyfriend routine again, but it seems I don't need to.

"You're here for Austin Grimm?" the nurse asks. He's in green scrubs with a grey zip-up hoodie. His wire-framed glasses are what I think social media is referring to as "slutty" these days, though nerds have never done much for me.

Blond athletes with thighs like tree trunks and a thing for hickeys, however . . .

"Yes, is he okay?"

"I'm glad you're here," the nurse says. "He's stable, but he's in rough shape. Broken ribs, collapsed lung, concussion, hairline fracture on his jaw, broken collarbone, ankle and wrist."

My stomach twists at the list. Some of them I guessed while we were sitting in the snow and mud. Others, though . . . a collapsed lung? Holy shit.

"But he's alive, right?"

His mouth twists right along with my guts. "We don't keep them if they're dead."

Maybe that's supposed to make me feel better? I know a big part of coping in the medical field is dark humour. But now I'm having visions of Austin's cold body in a vinyl bag or with a tag tied to one toe, and I want to start crying all over again.

The nurse walks me down the hall. The doors to each room are all closed. Austin's is at the end, and I have to take a breath before I enter. Boyfriend or no, the idea of what I'm about to see is uncomfortable.

The nurse puts a hand on my shoulder. "He'll need a lot of rest to heal. They'll be doing surgery to pin his leg and collarbone tomorrow. There's a tube in his chest to make sure he keeps breathing and his lung doesn't collapse again, and the swelling around his jaw means he won't be able to talk much, but you can speak to him. Let him know you're here."

He must give that speech a lot to frightened family members. He finishes with one more smile, this one a little more comforting than before, then he leaves.

The room is dark, with the curtains pulled. I expect beeping monitors or something, but all I get is a rasp of Grimm's breathing. His leg is propped up on several pillows and his arm is covered in bandages or a cast that's been wrapped in something. There's a bandage around his head too, and when I turn on a small light above his bed, the neck of his hospital gown has been pulled to one side, revealing a misshapen bruise so dark it's practically black over his collarbone. I'm almost afraid to breathe on him, much less touch him, but finally I pull the chair by the edge of the bed a little closer. Tentatively, I take his good hand, the one that isn't covered in a cast, and rub my thumb over his knuckles. It's the first time I've touched his skin since last night and the difference between now and then—between bone-deep fear and desperate hunger—is almost painful.

"Hey, buddy," I say, voice scratchy in my throat. "It's me. Zed. I mean, it's Bear. I mean . . ."

My face crumples as I start to cry. At least I'm by myself. The nurse has gone to look after other patients. My sobs are born from relief and sadness. Terror and regret, but also the tiniest amount of comfort. Despite the braces and casts, the tubes and IVs, he's okay. Alive at least. He's going to be okay.

Austin stirs, eyelids fluttering as he squints up at the overhead light. I remember the thing the nurse said about the concussion and turn it out again. He's not supposed to have bright lights, right? Instead, we sit in the dim room, with only faraway light from the hallway helping to illuminate us.

"Hey," I say again, running my hand across his knuckles,

trying to reassure myself. He stares up at the ceiling for a long time. "It's okay. We got help. See? I told you. It's okay. I'm here."

He shifts in the bed, face contorting in pain. His soft moan is nothing like the ones he made last night. People say there can be a fine line between pleasure and pain, but in this case, the difference is clear.

I stand, getting ready to find the nurse and ask about medication. This isn't the time to be precious about drug tests and performance enhancements. The season is over for all of us, and even if it wasn't, it's definitely over for Austin. I glance at him, battered and broken, weighed down by casts and the pain of his injuries. For a minute, something in my chest feels like it's about to tear into pieces. An echo of fear that it may not just be his season that's over but maybe his career. I've seen competitors come back from injury before, but this?

Let him take all the drugs he wants if it keeps him comfortable. The rest are questions for days when he can do things like sit up or breathe unassisted.

But as I go back to the door, looking for the nurse, a surprisingly strong hand grabs hold of my wrist. I have to bite down a yelp, but when I turn back, Austin's gaze is as determined as his grip on my arm. He shakes his head, the movement small so he doesn't upset his injuries.

"You want me to stay?" I ask.

He makes a jerky little nod.

"Do you need the nurse? More medication?"

Austin blinks a few times, but finally he makes another little shake of his head, though this one is followed by a wince.

I clasp my hand around his, licking my lips and trying to think what to say.

"You okay? Do you need anything? Morphine? An orgasm?" The questions tumble out in a barrage of nervous word vomit and I immediately feel like an idiot. A hand job is the last thing he needs right now; we both know that. I'm afraid to make him laugh. But even a small smile would help the lead weight that's tugging at my heart.

Austin frowns, but the expression is about confusion now, not pain. He lets go of my hand, making a swirling motion in the air, like he's writing something with a pen, or else casting a spell. When I don't react fast enough, he sighs heavily, then holds his hand up to his ear like he's talking on the phone, then points at me.

"My phone? You want my phone?"

He nods and his motion changes to jabbing at the air, maybe like he's badly typing a message.

I fumble for my phone, but manage to get it out and open the notes app, before setting it right in front of his extended finger. Watching him type is excruciating. He moves slowly, and every so often even the simple impact of his finger on the screen is enough to make him flinch. Finally, though, a question forms.

Race. I won?

I choke on a new sob.

"Don't worry about it. It was a stupid idea. I didn't think it would . . . that you would . . . who won doesn't matter."

But he frowns and punches some more at the phone.

Itly. Quali?

Then he points at me. It takes a second to decipher what he means.

"Did *I* qualify for the Olympics?"

He nods once, then watches me expectantly.

"No, I fell. You won. You're the one who qualified. Remember?"

He frowns some more, brows bunching toward the centre of his face. He points at himself, then makes a circular shape over his chest, which I finally realize is meant to be a medal. An Olympic medal.

"Yeah," I say. "You won. You're going to the Olympics. I fell. Didn't finish. Remember? You said . . ." The rest of the sentence dies in my throat. He asked about the race, and I assumed he meant our little match after the photoshoot. But if he doesn't remember that he qualified, did he mean yesterday's race? It feels like a lifetime ago.

"You remember the Big Final, right?" I ask. "You came first."

I expect him to smile. Maybe give me a thumbs-up. Instead, Austin stares upward, blinking rapidly. His chest rises and falls in time with the hiss of the breathing machine near his bedside, and I want so badly to put my hand on his chest like I did on the hillside, to make sure I could still feel his heartbeat, but I'm afraid of hurting him.

Finally, he gives a gentle shake of his head, and my breath stops for what feels like the hundredth time today.

"You don't remember the race?" A weird sensation shudders through my body and I mask it with a smile. "In that case, you were a disaster. Flamed out before qualis. It was a tragedy. Your worst performance this season. You're lucky you have me because I was awesome. First in every heat and then the Big Final . . ." My tale fades away, because he's watching me with the same direct gaze, but there's no laughter. No rolling his eyes at my blatant lies. I swallow a lump of dread that lodges in my throat. I could tell him anything. That Canada had been disqualified from all of sport. That aliens had landed on the mountaintop and abducted us. He doesn't seem to be able to tell the difference between fact and fiction.

I squeeze his hand a little tighter, then brush a hand over his forehead, like I did in the woods while we waited for help. His frown deepens.

"I love you, Grimm," I say, voice cracking slightly.

He raises his finger, tapping at the screen some more.

Lov Zed

Cold fear blankets my shoulders and I ask the question that will confirm the worry that gnaws at my guts.

"Do you remember last night? The bar? Karaoke? Do you remember . . ." My moment of bravery snuffs out and the question shrivels on my tongue. He's looking at me, brow still knit tight in confusion, but when I don't speak again, he shakes his head some more, and a single tear slips from his eye.

He doesn't remember. Any of it. He said he loved Zed. Not Bear.

And what does it matter? I'm being incredibly selfish. I want him to remember coming his brains out on my dick when he can't even breathe without a machine. Who cares about anything else?

I have to cough to clear my throat. "It's okay. It's fine." Not to worry. He's full of painkillers and other drugs. I'm lucky he remembers my name.

The lump rises painfully in my throat again and I swallow hard, but it won't go away. I can't breathe. It's like the panic attack in the hotel room. I clutch my hands tightly in my lap, forcing my face to stay neutral. Austin can't see what I'm feeling. Not now. Not like he is. He'll remember. When the drugs wear off and the pain subsides, he'll remember what happened. He said he's been in love with me for ages. He can't forget that.

My smile hurts as I watch him. Slowly, he lifts his hand, pointing again. I hold the phone for him as he types.

You stay

"Yeah," I say. "Yeah. I'm not going anywhere. Don't worry."

We sit in silence. His eyes flutter closed, which is good because it means he can't see me cry. It's more controlled than it was a minute ago. Soft snuffling sounds as tears slide over my cheeks. I should go. I wanted to see him and now I have. There's nothing I can do for him. But I can't walk away. So I sit there, holding his hand while he sleeps. Eventually, I sleep too. After everything, there's no way to keep it away forever. My head bobs up and down as I try to get comfortable in the chair, but every position is impossible. Somehow, I doze for a bit and dream about Austin. He's touching me. Kissing me. His hands roam over my body. I'm so hard. So needy. If he would keep going a little more, I would come, but every time I get close, he disappears, leaving me to call for him. Then he's back and we start over, but we never get to the climax that—

A soft sound jerks me awake. At first, in my sleepy brain, I think it's Austin, snuggled up against me and grinding gently as he silently asks for my body again. But then I blink and remember we aren't in the hotel room. We're somewhere entirely different and more awful.

Austin groans again, and it's not from pleasure. He's awake, but his face contorts and his body stiffens with pain. I can barely stand to look at him.

"Let me go get the nurse," I say. "I'll be right back."

But as I stumble to my feet, the overhead light clicks on, making me stagger backward. Before my vision can clear, a shaking, sobbing form throws itself at me.

"Cedric. Oh my god, Cedric. What happened?"

The nurse from before, the one with the slutty glasses, is standing in the doorway.

"Everything okay?" he asks, shutting the light off again.

"I think he needs something for the pain," I say, before turning my attention to the weeping woman in my arms.

It's Austin's mom. Donna. I've known her for more than half my life. She's driven me to races, fed me dinner. I know the smell of her house and the place in the back row of her minivan where I scratched the seat with a pole while packing up after a race in the Laurentians. I hid it with my coat for the whole drive home because I was sure she would make me pay for the damage, and I was a fourteen-year-old kid with no money because I'd spent it all on a new pair of ice blue skis for the winter. When I finally admitted what I'd let happen, she'd hugged me and told me she'd raised three children and scratched minivans came with the territory.

"It's all right," she said. "I could never be mad at you. You're like my own kid."

I squeeze her, repeating the same thing. It's all right. All right.

Finally, she lets me go to sit in the chair I just vacated. The nurse must have topped up Austin's morphine or whatever, because his face is relaxed again and his eyes closed.

"Where's Patrick?" I ask, looking back to the door like Austin's father might appear at any moment.

She shakes her head. "He couldn't make the drive. Not with his back the way it is. We'd have had to break the trip up and . . ." She looks up at me. Her whole face is puffy, like she's been crying for hours. From Ottawa to here is at least a six-hour drive with no stops. She must have got in the car almost immediately. "They called us this afternoon. They said there was an accident and that he was going into surgery." Her voice breaks as she stares at her son. After a few more minutes she holds out her hand, and I take it. She presses it to her cheek. "I'm so glad you were here, Cedric. So he didn't have to be alone."

My hand shakes in hers, but she doesn't let go. Suddenly I feel like I'm nine years old all over again. I want to tell her everything. How it's my fault. The race. That I didn't recognize his call for help right away. That I didn't have my phone. I want her to absolve me like she did with the stupid minivan, but this and that aren't even close to being the same. I may have ended Austin's racing career. She can't forgive me for that.

"I didn't want him to be alone," I say, voice wavering.

She squeezes me again. "Of course. You've always been his best friend."

I nod. That's me. Reliable best friend. Her other son, even if I have a family of my own.

As I stand by my best friend's side, with the woman closer to me than almost anyone besides my own parents, I've never felt lonelier in my entire life.

CHAPTER
NINE

Canadian Skier Austin Grimm in Hospital After Dangerous Ski Accident

Canadian ski cross star Austin Grimm is in hospital following a dangerous skiing accident. The 22-year-old from Orléans, Ontario, was near Birmingham, Maine, for a World Cup ski cross event, but was injured on Monday morning following a photoshoot for the outerwear brand Apex.

"The shoot was over and Austin and some of his teammates and friends were headed back to the lodge when there was a crash," says Freestyle Ski Canada spokesperson Tara Parker. Parker further confirmed that Grimm suffered a broken jaw, broken collarbone, cracked ribs, a collapsed lung and liver laceration, as well as fractures to one wrist and ankle.

The accident is a tragic finish to what had been a spectacular weekend for Grimm, where he won the World Cup ski cross event hosted at the Holiday River ski resort. This was Grimm's second victory on the World Cup circuit this year and fifth top-three finish. His performance at Holiday River secured him a spot to represent Canada in ski cross during next year's Olympic Games in Milano-Cortina, Italy. Whether he will be able to compete now is unclear.

"It's too early to speculate on the future of Austin's athletic career," says Canada Ski team doctor, Joseph Wallace. "He has a great medical team looking after him in the US and we look forward to continuing his recovery once he's back home in Canada."

No confirmation was given as to the exact circumstances of the accident. The photoshoot occurred on a part of the Holiday River ski area that had been closed for private use, but terrain conditions were deemed to be safe for all skiers.

———

Excerpt for Fall Line Podcast episode 189 interview, August 29, 2025, between host George McNally and Austin Grimm

McNally: So you're lying in the snow, broken bones, not sure how long until help arrives. What are you thinking in that moment?

Grimm: To be honest, I don't really know. That whole day, and even parts of the day before are gone.

McNally: What do you mean "gone"?

Grimm: I mean I don't remember them.

McNally: Wait, wait. Are we talking about amnesia?

Grimm: Maybe? Something like that. Also, I was on a lot of painkillers that day, so along with the concussion, there was some . . . interference.

McNally: Yeah. Yeah, I get that. It had to be awful, though, right? You nearly died.

Grimm: I don't know about that. I remember waking up in the hospital and not knowing where I was or how I got there. For the first few days, I thought the fall had happened during the World Cup race. It was only after that I understood it had happened the next day. I have to give big thanks to the Holiday River ski patrol who got me off the snow so fast. And all my doctors and surgeons at the hospital.

McNally: How many surgeries did you have?

Grimm: There's a screw in my wrist. Plate in my ankle. They had to go in twice because my lung kept collapsing. It was a lot.

McNally: It's a miracle you're alive. And yet here you are, five months later. And you're talking about competing? Most people might go through something like that and say, "You know what? That's enough for me." No one would blame you if you left the national team and decided you wanted to be a dog walker or something.

Grimm: Well, I do love dogs. But I love skiing more. I don't know who I'd be if I couldn't ski anymore. And race. I've been working hard with my coaches, physiotherapists, and trainers to get ready for competition.

McNally: For the World Cup? The Olympics?

Grimm: We'll see. I don't want to get back on the mountain before my body is ready. I've been through a lot in the last five months. I need to know I can take an impact if I fall. That I'm strong enough to be able to keep up with the best in the world.

McNally: And maybe even pass them?

Grimm: That's the plan, yeah. I want to go out and race the best race I can, but winning is nice sometimes too.

McNally: Winning at the Olympics?

Grimm: Two months ago the doctors weren't sure I'd be able to do much more than walk without pain, so everything else is a bonus day.

———

Excerpt from Total Sports Network article, December 11, 2025

Newcomer Harrison Qualifies for Olympics in Ski Cross

In a surprising performance, newcomer Kage Harrison has qualified to represent Canada at the winter games in Milano-Cortina, after finishing second in the 2025/26 Ski Cross World

Cup season's inaugural event at Val Thoreau, France, this week-end. The twenty-year-old from Calgary had only joined the senior men's team for last year's 2024/25 season and is an unexpected qualifier for the upcoming Olympic team.

"I knew I was in good shape before the start of the Big Final," Harrison said. "I'd been skiing well all weekend. I just had to go out there and keep it up and I knew I had a shot."

Harrison placed second behind Norwegian skier Anders Flaska. Canadian three-time ski cross champion Matthieu Girard came fourth in the Big Final, and veteran teammate Andrew Spinner placed sixth in the Small Final. The other Canadian at the event, Cedric Berard, failed to move out of the preliminary heats and placed thirtieth out of thirty-two competitors.

With only two months left before the start of the Olympics, the Canadian men's ski cross team is facing uncertainty. Harrison and Girard have qualified, along with teammate Austin Grimm, who qualified last season. However, Grimm suffered a serious injury while skiing outside competition and his return to the World Cup circuit and the Olympics this year is in question.

"We're hoping Austin will be able to join us. He's making good progress with our trainers and coaches, but we still need the all-clear from team doctors," says Canadian ski cross head coach Ivan Bondarenko.

If Grimm is able to compete, that leaves one spot on the Canadian Olympic ski cross roster, and only four more events for either Spinner or Berard to accumulate the necessary points to qualify.

Skiing Canada Sports Brief, January 19, 2026

Spinner Punches Olympic Ticket

In a dramatic Big Final at this weekend's World Cup Ski Cross event at San Mosino, Italy, Canadian ski cross mainstay Andrew Spinner narrowly beat out teammate Cedric Berard to scoop up the final remaining spot on the Canadian ski cross team for the men's event in Milano-Cortina next month. Spinner finished second and Berard finished third in Sunday's final. Berard only needed to finish in the top three to make the team, but with only one spot left on the roster and Spinner finishing this year's qualifying period with more World Cup points, Berard finds himself on the outside looking in.

"It's disappointing," said Berard after the race, "to work for something and not get it. But Andrew's an amazing competitor and a great teammate. I'm really happy for him and everyone else. They've all worked really hard to get where they are."

Spinner, set to appear in his second Olympics after missing the 2022 games in Beijing due to injury, echoed Berard's sentiments.

"We've all worked hard this season, and Cedric and I knew that it was make or break going into this weekend. But all you can do is focus on the next turn and the next race."

The other Canadians at the event included Matthieu Girard, who finished eighth, and Kage Harrison, who came eleventh in quarter-final action. Fellow teammate Austin Grimm was slated to race, after staging what some are calling a miraculous comeback following a tragic injury last year after the end of the World Cup season. However, Grimm was a last-minute withdrawal for this weekend's event.

"My doctors said I'm ready," Grimm said on Friday. "But we're being careful. I've been doing practice runs and feeling good. I'll be ready to go by the time we get to Italy."

———

World Ski News Article, February 1, 2026

Canadian Ski Cross Team in Turmoil After Drug Test Bomb

The Canadian men's ski cross team is facing yet another shakeup only days ahead of the start of the Olympic Games in Milano-Cortina, Italy. The composition of the men's team has been in flux since 23-year-old World Cup winner Austin Grimm experienced a major accident in the off-season. Although he had already qualified to represent his country in Milan, his spot on the team was in question for most of the last ten months while he worked to come back from several major fractures and more.

Now, although Grimm is being celebrated as a miracle comeback story, it's his teammate Andrew Spinner who is in the spotlight following a positive drug test result after last weekend's World Cup race at San Mosino.

"There's been an error," says Team Canada ski cross head coach Ivan Bondarenko. "We are confident in our trainers and athletes. Andrew has been very serious about not taking any kind of medication that would jeopardize his qualification at the Olympics."

Spinner wouldn't be the first athlete to get caught up in a pre-games drug scandal, even inadvertently. Past Canadians who were suddenly disqualified from competition over a positive drug test result include ski jumper Naomi Mackenzie-Miller and short track speed skater Olivier LaRochelle. Both were later reinstated when the results were shown to be a lab error in Mackenzie-Miller's case and the result of a mislabeled over-the-counter allergy medication LaRochelle had taken before a World Tour event.

With Spinner's appeal before the Sports Commission but so little time before the Olympics kick off, it's uncertain if he will be cleared to compete. In the event he is not, Canadian teammate Cedric Berard was able to score enough World Cup Points to compete in ski cross in Spinner's place.

CHAPTER
TEN

WHEN I WAS A KID, I remember watching the Olympic opening ceremonies in Vancouver on TV with my family. There were fireworks. And dancers. Then the athletes entered. I was amazed. I had no idea there were so many countries in the world. And when the Canadians walked in at the very end? I knew right then that was what I wanted from my life. I wanted to walk in that parade in my team uniform, waving a little red and white flag while smiling at the camera. Representing my country. Standing with my teammates. Being celebrated for doing something most people would never even hope to be able to do.

My experience of the first day at the Olympics is completely different from that childhood dream.

For one, I arrive the day after the opening ceremonies. And I'm alone, flying in on a commercial flight jammed with tourists hoping to catch a glimpse of their favourite athlete or finally see their favourite sport live.

"If you want the spot, you have to come now."

That's what Ivan said when he called me the day before yesterday. I was at home, getting ready to head out to the gym. Just because I didn't qualify doesn't mean I get time off. There are still five more World Cup events after the games, and with my shitty start to the season, I have a lot of ground to make up.

But then the phone rang and my week changed.

I feel bad for Spinner. There's no way he took something intentionally. He doesn't even drink coffee and talks about sugar the way my mom talks about heroin—if she ever talked about heroin. But whatever happened, he's stuck until the commission finishes their investigation, and no amount of me graciously going "but it's not my team spot to take" will change the fact he'll have to wait four more years to get another shot at the Olympics.

After my anonymous flight to Italy, I expect to be greeted with little or no ceremony at the airport. Ivan promised there would be a driver to pick me up, but instead, the second I step through the sliding doors after customs and baggage claim, I'm swarmed with shouted questions and camera flashes that make me shield my eyes as I try to understand what's going on. The questions come in what feels like a million different languages, but finally a few in English and French filter through.

"Did you speak to Andrew Spinner before you left Canada?"

"How do you feel about Austin Grimm's comeback?"

"Do you think you have a shot at the podium given your late arrival?"

I blink, mouth falling open. In between physical training sessions, we're occasionally given media training too, and I know the guys who made the Olympics had a more intensive session in the last few weeks before they left. But since I was on the outside looking in, I only know the basics. Stay positive, focus on the future, don't comment on anything controversial. Andrew's situation is clearly off the table. But Austin? I'm not sure.

An arm slips through mine, pulling me swiftly through the throng of reporters.

"Keep your head down," Tara says. During the off-season, she made the transition from brands to media relations, and while I'll always be a little afraid of her, right now I'm so grateful to see her.

"I thought I was looking for a driver."

"Plans change. The commission denied Andrew's appeal. Said his test result was valid."

"What?" The idea is unthinkable.

"It's bullshit, but the media got hold of it while you were in the air. The whole team is in damage-control mode. No talking to reporters unless I tell you specifically."

My head spins, partially with disbelief, mostly with jet lag. Because I was flying on short notice to what is currently one of the most popular destinations in the world, the route I wound up taking went from Montreal to London to Paris to Rome to Milan. I have been awake for close to thirty-six hours because even though I knew I should sleep on the plane, my brain would not shut down. I was going to the Olympics. The season was a disaster and I had basically made my peace with this not being my year. Even when I finally managed a podium finish, Andrew was there to finish ahead of me and take the last spot. So for Ivan to call me less than two days before the opening ceremonies and tell me to get my ass on a plane to Italy was the beginning of the wildest whirlwind I've experienced since . . .

"No reporters. Got it." Suits me. At this point, I'm so tired I'm not even sure I'd answer questions in English.

The freestyle ski events are being held in Livigno. The maps app on my phone said it's about a three-hour drive, but that didn't consider the absolute traffic nightmare that is thousands of athletes and team staff descending on northern Italy all at once, not to mention the spectators, media, dignitaries, and more. The clock on my phone says it takes closer to six, though I don't remember much of it. Tara's picked me up in a sleek black van, the kind meant to transport six to eight people from one place to another. I stretch out in the very back row of seats and try not to puke as we wind our way up twisting roads to the Alps.

"The team has training this afternoon," Tara says as we pull into the town of Livigno. I've skied in races in the region before, but never here. It looks like most European ski towns, and we stop in front of a massive hotel with wood exterior and cute little balconies that backs onto a frozen lake. "Ivan will want you there, but he said if you're not up to ski, you can at least walk the run to get a feel for the terrain."

I swallow hard. I can barely keep my eyes open. But arriving late like I am means I'm already at a disadvantage from the other competitors who have had time to acclimate to the altitude and familiarize themselves with the course. The races start in three days, so every minute counts. I may not have qualified for the Olympics in the usual manner, but I'm here now and anyone who thinks I'm going to be easy pickings in the qualifying heat is kidding themselves.

"I'll be there," I say.

Volunteers appear from the hotel to help unload my gear, promising in broken English to get it to the equipment team. Another tries to take my suitcase and it leaves me feeling naked, so I hold it tight and promise him I can manage. As I head for the main doors, they open and three men emerge. They're all dressed in a variety of practice race suits, but each is wearing the signature red and white toque that was provided to all the Team Canada athletes. They laugh and jostle each other in easy camaraderie, while my suitcase falls to the snow and my feet root themselves in place.

It's Matthieu, Kage . . . and Austin. They all take another second before they spot me and for a sec it's like a standoff in an old cowboy movie, before Kage hoots and slides over the snow.

"Zed! You made it! That's so awesome!" He practically tackles me in his enthusiasm to greet me, but I manage to hold onto him. He's had a good year. Skied hard and made people take notice. Even if I was pissed at my own performance at that first race this year, I was happy for his qualification.

"Cedric," Matthieu says, clapping me on the shoulder. "Bienvenue."

I give him a tight smile as I gently shrug Kage off.

"Hey, Zed."

Austin's soft voice makes my heart twist uncomfortably.

"Hey, Grimm. I told you we'd make the Olympics."

The silence that falls between the four of us feels dense. Kage and Matthieu are suddenly very interested in the clouds that float high overhead in a blue sky. Austin scratches at his hair through the side of his toque. Sometime over the summer he cut it off, losing the long strands I tugged at while we . . .

"Where's Spinner?" I ask, because why not make everything more uncomfortable?

Matthieu clears his throat. "They made him leave the village. He's staying with family somewhere else."

I bite my lip. The others throw a few accusing glances at Tara, who's chatting with someone in an official-looking STAFF winter coat. This whole thing is fucked up. When the dust settles, they're going to clear him and while none of this is my fault, I'm the one who took his place.

"Ivan's waiting," Kage says, nudging Matthieu. They nod at me and head for the van I've just vacated. Austin lingers, hands in his pockets.

"You okay?" he asks. "How was the trip?"

"Yeah, fine," I say, stuffing my hands in my pockets too. Silence drops between us like an avalanche. Austin clears his throat and scratches at his jaw. He looks like he's about to say something, but then the quiet is shattered as a group of Australian athletes in their green and yellow team gear emerge from the hotel, laughing and chatting as they pass us. Austin's gaze follows them and when he swings back to me, whatever thought he was about to voice is gone. He gives me a quick smile and a nod, and follows after Kage and Matthieu who are waiting by the van.

When he's gone and the van pulls away, I let out a long slow breath, then right my suitcase. He looked good. Ready. The media is calling his comeback a miracle, and for the average person it would be. But we're not average people. It was Austin's literal job, his only responsibility, to get back into competition form. The team threw every professional they could at helping his recovery.

All day every day. That's all he had to do, and it shows. Physically, he's in as good shape as ever.

Our friendship, though . . . and anything else we were going to be. That's another story.

The hotel is nice. It's got a vintage feel. Just like I pictured myself among smiling teammates at the opening ceremonies and instead got a solo flight across what felt like half of Europe, somehow I imagined the athlete's village would be a complex of gleaming brand-new buildings, but in the modern era of sustainable games, it's more about repurposing existing properties. The Canadian team is staying on the top two floors. I'm relieved to discover I'm rooming with Matthieu, not Austin. So relieved, in fact, that once the door shuts behind me, my knees buckle and I slump onto the empty bed closest to the bathroom.

This has not been my season in every way that matters. Poor performance. Qualifying for the Olympics based on someone else's misfortune. None of this is the way I imagined all those years Austin and I were coming up.

And the worst part about it is, I can't even tell Austin about any of it.

I pull my phone out of my pocket and text my parents, letting my mom know I landed safely. It's only mid-morning back in Ottawa, so she replies immediately, sending messages in fast succession.

How was the flight?

How's the snow?

How are you feeling?

My thumbs hover over the screen, debating if I even want to reply.

Did you see Austin? We saw him on TV last night at the opening ceremonies. He looked great!

Yeah, no. I'm not answering that. The question is too loaded and any answer I give her will only lead her to pressing for more details. My parents tried to come to Italy with me, but it turned out to be impossible. With my short-notice call up, we were lucky to get me a flight. Booking airfare for Mom and Dad too would have involved selling one of the cars out of their driveway. My mom said they'd find a way. I'm not holding my breath.

Dad and I are so proud of you two.

My hand jerks around the phone and I put it down. That's the last thing she said to me when I called from the airport too. That she and my dad are proud of me. And Austin. We will always be a pair in their minds, just like Donna knew I'd be at the hospital when she arrived last year. Mom doesn't look at my late arrival at the Olympics as anything other than all my hard work paying off. She sees it as the inevitable conclusion of all the years she and Donna swapped carpool duties and she stood in the freezing January cold to cheer me and Austin on while we were still skiing alpine.

But this year has been . . . weird. Austin was in the hospital in Maine for close to a couple weeks. I stayed for a few days, even after the team left, but he was pretty out of it. Eventually, Patrick finally arrived to be with Donna, and the ICU staff started dropping hints about Austin needing quiet and rest. They clearly meant there were too many of us around, and what was I supposed to do? Tell Donna to take a hike?

After I got home, I texted a few times, but the concussion meant he wasn't allowed to use screens for a while, and even once he was, he still only had one good hand, needed multiple surgeries, and was loopy from the pain meds. I called once, and he sounded good, but then when I called the next day, he didn't remember speaking to me the day before.

Still, all of that is excuses, because the real problem was I didn't know what to say. "How are you doing?" seemed bad when I already knew what the answer was. And, "Hey, do you remember riding my dick until neither of us could practically walk?" didn't feel like the kind of thing to put in a text to your best friend when it's unclear if he'll ever be able to walk properly ever again.

So, after the first couple weeks, I mostly said nothing. Austin got discharged, but the team doctors agreed he'd do best at a private sports rehab facility in British Columbia. So even during the off-season, while we were doing dry land training, gym sessions, and keeping fit with things like mountain biking, Austin wasn't there. When we did communicate, it was mostly in memes, social media links, and occasionally gossip about teammates and competitors. Those things felt safest, and it was easy to hide behind "sorry, I've been busy with training." So we never actually said anything important to each other.

I don't know what happened. Somehow I went from imagining a perfect future for the two of us to barely being able to speak to my best friend. The guy who blew my mind in bed and promised me forever, then immediately forgot about all of that and nearly died.

But hey, after everything, at least I get to prove to the world I'm the best ski cross athlete on the hill right now? Or I get to try anyway. Once upon a time, Austin and I made a plan. Train hard. No distractions. If you fall, get back up and do it again. We dreamed of standing on top of the podium together.

I'm not sure if together is still on the table. Austin thinks we're friends . . . maybe . . . and I know we could be so much more. But, regardless, the rest of the plan still stands.

The pillow is very inviting. I could close my eyes and worry about all this later. But I've got three days to get my head on straight before competition starts. There's no time to sleep . . . or brood about how I'm ever going to salvage my relationship with Austin. He said once he'd wanted to wait until after the games. This is exactly what he was talking about. And whether he knows it or not, now I get a second chance to stick to the plan.

It's time to compete.

CHAPTER
ELEVEN

THE CONDITIONS on the mountain are perfect. There's been a lot of snow this winter, but nothing new in the last few weeks, which has given the stuff that's already fallen time to be compacted down under skis and the grooming equipment the resort uses to maintain terrain. The air is cold and the sun is bright, so it's easy to see the dips and shadows where the pitch changes, even before the course team has put down the stripes of spray paint meant to indicate the start of jumps or the bank of a turn.

It's absolutely perfect, and I am a mess.

It begins where all races do: at the start. Austin, Matthieu, and Kage are doing drills. Ski cross is different from most other ski events in that the races are done with four competitors on the course at a time, and our starting gates have handles. They're small horizontal bars that you grab onto, so you can rock yourself backward, then launch yourself forward when the barrier comes down, sort of the way swimmers will use the edge of the starting platform for leverage to get into the water faster. I take my place next to the others, gripping the bars tight while making sure my poles are pointed behind me and out of the way. I take a deep breath, letting the tension pull through my shoulders as I bend my knees low and lean into the tough plastic of my boots. I've started from gates like these thousands of times. It all comes down to breath and timing. The trainer counts down the seconds until the start and as the barrier drops I pull myself forward, getting ready to launch onto the course . . . only to find myself faceplanting in the snow as something below my shin snaps.

What the fuck?

The guys, only a few metres beyond as they rock over the first set of rollers on the course, look back to find me sprawled on the ground. Kage hoots. Matthieu puts his hands to his hips, leaning against his poles. Austin skates back toward me.

"You okay?" he asks.

"Cedric, what the hell was that?" Ivan calls from above the gates. I roll onto my back, swinging my skis wide to avoid snagging them in the snow. I didn't even fall hard enough to pop the bindings, but it's okay. My ego is still plenty bruised.

Also, one of the buckles is hanging off the front of my boot like a dangling tree limb waiting to fall on an unsuspecting jogger. The damn thing must have popped off under the pressure of the start.

"Fine," I say, getting back up to my feet. "Just a technical malfunction."

"Do you want to walk the course instead?" he asks.

My jaw tightens. I don't need to be treated differently than the others. My late arrival and my spill already have me feeling like a bit of an outsider while the three of them are clustered together, chatting and leaning against the tops of their poles while they wait for me to recover.

"Just let me get fresh boots."

By the time new boots are brought over from where the equipment team has staged themselves, the rest of my own team has already moved on from starts and is traveling the course slowly, stopping at each turn and feature to discuss lines, tactics, and strategy. Inspection like this is usually my favourite part of the pre-competition days. A chance to really break down the run into its individual parts and look for every possible chance to make up time or gain the lead over the rest of the pack. Especially for a run I've never done before, this is where the idea of my victory starts to form. Piece by piece I build a winning run, while the people I spend my whole winter with—and most of the off-season too—do the same. A shared goal, even if there can only be one first place.

But today, instead of joining in the conversation, I'm left rushing through the components with one of the assistant coaches. We examine turns and consider things like pitch and spacing between jumps. Hailey, the assistant coach in question, is good. She knows the snow almost as well as Ivan. But there's something calming about talking it through with everyone. We may be competing against each other, but at the end of the day we're still a team. And yes, I'm a sudden and unexpected addition to this particular version of the line up, but I wasn't expecting to feel so much like it.

When I'm done, the others are waiting for me.

"All set?" Ivan asks.

I blink, my poor jet lagged brain trying to follow his question. I fail.

"For what?"

"Pursuits." Kage's grin is excited.

I groan. The desire to tap out and head back to the hotel is extreme, but my opportunities to prepare are limited. I can sleep when I get back to Canada. So instead I clack my poles together and push off toward the chairlift.

"Let's do it."

Pursuits are like mini races. Instead of four men on the run, it's only two. On its face, it's about who can get to the bottom fastest, like any other trip down the mountainside. From a training perspective, it's more about getting a feel for the course even when your ideal line isn't available because someone else is already on it or is so far up your ass you have to make changes to your plan.

We take turns. Kage and Austin go first. Matthieu and I wait for our signal.

"I'm glad you're here," he says.

I wrinkle my nose beneath my goggles. "Pretty sure Spinner would disagree with that sentiment."

He makes a distinctly French-Canadian sound that is equal parts amusement and denial. "Andrew will have his moment. This was supposed to be your season. It's good you found a way, after everything."

Maybe it's gamesmanship. He's trying to get into my head before we take our turn down the hill. Maybe it's his version of sympathy, but all I can think is "after everything," I'm the one who blew my shot, and that no one here even knows how far "everything" goes. If I couldn't talk to Austin about what happened, I wasn't going to kiss and tell with anyone else either.

Ivan whistles and we take our positions in the gate. My boots hold together this time, at least. Matthieu takes the lead quickly and I let him have it. That's not the way pursuits work. It really should be a race, but my mind is elsewhere. My body goes through the motion of taking the turns and keeping my hands low on the straightaways, but my head is all over the map. A million places, in fact. Part of me thinks I'm still on the plane. Another part is standing on the sidelines in San Mosino, watching Andrew celebrate his qualification and knowing that spot could have been mine if I'd gotten myself together. But the problem is there's a huge part of me that's still sitting among the trees, desperately begging Austin not to die on me while we wait for help, and a further part that's still in bed with him, listening as he talks about the future like it's already a done deal. If only he could see us now. So much for the done deal.

By the time we reach the bottom, Matthieu's got a good distance between us, and when I cross the line, he's already stopped and scowling at me.

"What?" I ask, glancing around me. The base is busy, with other teams clustered around, talking strategy, checking times, and prepping equipment. No one seems at all interested in my abysmal performance.

Matthieu makes another French-Canadian noise, this one all exasperation and annoyance. But instead of saying anything, he simply shakes his head and skis back to the lift for another ride to the top. It's fine. I know what he's thinking. If I'm not even going to try, what am I doing here?

We ride up in silence. Chair lifts have always been a weird social microcosm. Austin and I had some serious conversations as teens while riding the lift at weekend practices and races. We talked about school, family, and our sexualities. Austin told me with trembling words about how he'd kissed Ridley Haynes, a boy in his geography class, at his first school dance, and how when he'd gotten home he'd had to jerk off three times before his lingering erection had gone down enough he could go to bed. Years later, I told him how I thought we should skip university and focus on making the senior team.

On this particular ride, Matthieu and I are silent. Nothing personal. Keep it focused on the race.

Today, we say nothing.

The next pursuit is with Kage. I expect Ivan to put me with Austin, but when he says Kage's name instead, I shoot him a look and all I get in reply is a thin press of lips that is wordless head coach speak for *don't fuck with me*, so I get in the gate next to Kage and we go. My run is better than the last one until the second to last jump, where I hit the back of it awkwardly and find my arms windmilling through the air in a desperate attempt to keep my balance. I land badly and too far downhill. Kage is already several seconds ahead of me, but he still cheers like I've set a new record as I come over the line.

"That was awesome," he says as we ride up together. "So awesome, right? I mean, obviously not you. That jump was ugly. Like, super gnarly. That's the one that Ivan said we should—" He pauses, giving me a glance. "Oh right. You weren't there for that conversation because of your boot. Anyway, he said—" He chatters in an endless stream of consciousness fueled entirely by excited adrenaline. I nod, and listen, silently wondering if my late arrival means I'm going to get the short end of the team stick right up until the start of competition. But Ivan wouldn't do that. It's not his fault I was a late substitution or that my buckle broke. I'm creating conspiracies where there aren't any, and I already have enough going on.

For example, being able to make eye contact with Austin when Ivan inevitably pairs us for the final pursuit is a challenge all on its own.

"You ready?" Austin asks, grinning playfully as he holds out a gloved hand for me to bump. It's a ritual we've had for years. A reminder that even though only one of us can win, we're in this together. But my smile feels wooden and when I go to bump him back, I miss, knocking against empty nothingness before my hand falls uselessly to my side again. Austin only laughs. "Holy air ball. You sure you're up for this?"

I roll my eyes. Today is the first time we've been on the hill together since . . . then. That awful day. I don't know why he's being so casual about it. My knees nearly buckle as I slide into the gate and my knuckles ache where I grip the handles too hard. I'm already behind before the barrier drops and my poles clang against the metal, meaning they're in the wrong position as I try to push my way through the opening rollers. The whole thing is terrible and I'm going to hear about it from Ivan later. By the time the course opens up into the first pitch, Austin's already way ahead of me. He moves so fast, body position perfect. The whole point of a pursuit is to practice with a competitor trying to over-take you. But I'm so far behind he might as well be skiing alone.

He's like poetry in motion. Austin always had flawless tech-nique. I got through the early years of our training on speed because I wasn't afraid of anything. Austin always had a sense for the snow and the hill that meant he could find a line no one else knew was there. It seems, despite everything, he hasn't lost that gift. I tuck down, making up enough ground that I don't lose him from view as he hits the next jump and drifts downhill. I wince when he hits the ground again, remembering impacts in the forest that shattered bones. Never mind I didn't see the accident. I've dreamed about it so many times since then, I know every tree stump and rock he hit between the time I looked back and he wasn't there and the moment I found him crumpled on the ground.

"Wooo!" Austin lets out a long, joyful cry as we fly down the mountain, and for a minute everything is like it's always been. Friends. Brothers. The two of us headed toward victory, side by side, or as close as we can be. But as quickly as that joy pours over me like warm water, it turns to ice when his cry turns into an alarmed sound. His left ski lifts off the ground and his arms swing. He's going over. There isn't even anything here to make him fall. No turn, no jump. The snow is perfectly even, but he's wheeling and leaning and my heart swells so hard in my throat for a minute I can't breathe and my vision goes black. Not again. I can't see him get hurt again.

Then he's sliding over the line, both skis back on the ground and he cheers for himself, arms raised over his head in celebration. He's elated, and his happiness hits me in the gut worse than any rock or tree stump ever could.

"What the hell is wrong with you?" I ask, pulling up to a stop in front of him, so close he has to stop short, throwing his weight onto his poles to keep from crashing into me.

"What are you talking about?" he asks, but the lingering smile in his eyes only makes me angrier.

"Is this a joke to you? We're days from competition and you're fucking around on the hill?"

Austin's brow pinches together. His face scrunches up and he tugs his buff down, so it hangs around his neck.

"Fucking around?" he asks, pursing his lips in confusion. The gesture highlights how his mouth is slightly lopsided in a way it didn't used to be. I can't see it, but somewhere along his jaw is a scar where they had to cut him open after the hairline fracture in his jaw got bigger and they went in to screw it back together. I wasn't there, of course, but I heard about it, because along with team gossip, my mom and Donna have basically created a two-woman colour commentary team. They've documented and relayed every single detail of his surgeries and rehab. Honestly, I'm surprised they didn't start a podcast, because every phone call I've had with my parents since the accident has included what I've come to think of as "the Austin Segment" where Mom tells me about her latest conversation with Donna and all the updates from his doctors and therapists. I'm sure she meant it to feel comforting to hear that Austin was making progress, and maybe she was surprised I hadn't heard it directly from him, but every time she talked to me about it, it let me relive the terror of finding him and only amplified the sense of how separate we've been ever since.

"You nearly fell," I say, anger rising inside me.

"That?" Austin shrugs carelessly. "It was nothing. Didn't matter anyway, with how far behind me you were. I had lots of time to recover." He bangs playfully at my shins with a pole, which should be a signal that it's time for a little friendly rough-housing, but his lack of concern sends me flying into a rage. I swing a pole at him, but instead of aiming low like he did, I swat at his arm, hard enough it might bruise, even with his layers of clothing. He gasps, hopping back as his eyes get big in shock. "What the fuck?"

"Exactly. What the fuck, Austin? This is serious."

"You think I don't know that?" His voice rises, and my blood goes with it. Maybe a fight is what we need. Get it all out there. "After everything I've been through to get here?"

"After everything *you've* been through?" Only my feet still clipped into my bindings keep me from launching myself at him.

"Hey, what's going on?" Hailey calls behind me, reminding me we're not alone. You're never alone at events like this. Except for once, when it was only the two of us in a hotel room. That's where it all went sideways and now we're here.

I'm breathing hard, and the cold is making my nose run, but a screaming match right now will only land us on Ivan's shit list, along with tonight's highlight reel for any sports network who happens to have a reporter roving practices for potential stories, and more than a few social media feeds. Now isn't the time, like it hasn't been the time for months and months. I spit a goober of snot into the snow, closer to the tips of Austin's skis than I probably should. He slides a few more inches back, head tilted to one side before finally his expression clouds and he laughs once.

"Fine. Whatever, Zed. Sorry we interrupted your two-week vacation." Then he pushes off, sliding past me and heading back toward the lift.

We don't say anything on the ride back up. We don't even ride together. I watch the back of his head from my chair, while my whole body shakes with fury.

I WISH I could say things are awkward when we get back to the athlete accommodations, but they aren't really anything. Kage and Matthieu keep up a steady stream of conversation in the van on the way into the village. Austin's watching something on his phone. No one so much as acknowledges my presence. When we enter the hotel, I go straight to my room. There's another string of text messages from my parents, and even a couple from Donna. Mostly they ask how my day was, how Austin's doing, and what our plans are for tonight. Like I have any plans besides bed. I strip out of my clothes, and I'm basically asleep before my head even hits the pillow. After two whirlwind days of traveling and this afternoon's training, I have nothing left in me.

When I wake up again, it's dark. Matthieu is in the other bed, snoring gently. I check my phone and it's three in the morning. Nine o'clock at home. Jet lag sucks. I roll over, firmly shutting my eyes and try to go back to sleep, but even though Matthieu's snoring is barely more than a loud exhale, it seems like the noisiest thing I have ever experienced. Twenty minutes later, I'm stumbling around with only my phone flashlight to help me find my bags. I slip into sweats and shoes, and let myself out of the room.

I'm not the only one awake. The main floor of the hotel isn't exactly busy, but there are more than a dozen people milling around. Some are in various national team apparel, but most are in faded and worn athletic gear. We're all wound too tight to lie in bed. A few have found food, sipping on coffee and small plates of fruit. The hotel must be prepared for the kind of hours we keep. Two women walk past me, red faced and breathing hard. One mops sweat from her brow with a towel.

"The gym?" I ask and she points down a hallway.

The gym was probably a conference room or something. Big halogen lights illuminate the space, but the walls are panelled in golden wood, and the wooden floors have been covered in protective rubber mats to keep the weight racks and cardio equipment from scratching them. Half the machines are in use, but I find a treadmill, pop in my headphones, and set a gentle pace.

I used to hate running. When we got to the point in our teenage racing careers where it wasn't enough to show up on Saturdays and ski as fast as we possibly could down the hill, I was so disappointed to find out that our dryland training involved running. If I wanted to be a runner, I'd have joined track and field. These days, though, it's not so bad. When it's warm enough, I tend to stick to mountain biking for cardio, but sometimes a few kilometres on a treadmill are what I need to get my mind to go blank.

Also, it's annoying that I still think of me and Austin and our racing careers—both teenage and otherwise—as a "we." I don't even know what we are anymore. I'm the one who's making things weird, but it's not like he reached out to me much while he was rehabbing in BC either. The occasional selfie. A text sent after I'd gone to bed because west coast time is three hours behind. Beyond that, pretty much everything I knew was mom-to-mom gossip and the things I could find out from news articles and ski media like podcasts. It was as though Austin had decided we weren't a "we" anymore, when only weeks and months earlier he'd been promising he was going to turn our Olympic dream into some gooey love-swept confession.

Like he's ready to prove my point, as I start to slow the treadmill again, feeling more grounded than I have in days, the door to the gym swings open, and Austin walks in, followed by a couple trainers. It's after four now and the gym is getting busier. It's not uncommon for athletes at our level to be up at five on a competition day, and that plus jet lag means we're all keeping weird hours. I catch Austin's entry out of the corner of my eye, but either he doesn't notice me or else he does but he's still pissed about yesterday, because he and the trainers go to one of the benches on the other side of the room. One of them pulls out some resistance bands, while Austin sits. He's in shorts, compression leggings and a T-shirt, which gives me a better opportunity to look at him as I step off the treadmill than I had yesterday while he was in all his outerwear. At first glance he looks good. Like he always did. Strong chest, thick thighs. His forearms are muscled, with tendons and veins stretching beneath his skin. He looks like he did that night in my bed. Fit. Ready for anything.

But then the trainers start whatever regimen they've planned for him and it only takes a minute before he grimaces. It's not a face made from exertion, the one we all make as we push our bodies to their limits. It's pain. A restriction. Something that doesn't bend or stretch the way it used to and even the small reminder of pain I only witnessed is enough to have me recoiling back so suddenly my heel bangs against the treadmill frame, and I have to put a hand out to keep from falling over in front of the world's best snowboard and ski cross racers. The sound of the treadmill rattling is enough to make Austin look up, and when our eyes meet, I feel like a prey animal who's suddenly been spotted by an entire pack of wolves who haven't eaten properly in weeks. Never mind that his expression is more confused than hungry. I can't be here. I mutter an apology to no one and hurry out of the gym.

So, that went well. When I get back to the room, Matthieu is already awake.

"Work out?" he asks as I enter. I only manage a grunt before I shut myself in the bathroom, rattling soap and shampoo bottles together as I make a big production of showering. By the time I'm out, he's gone. I get dressed more slowly. Take some time to stretch properly after rushing so quickly out of the gym.

I'm being ridiculous, aren't I? Except I don't know how to turn it off. Once upon a time, everything seemed so clear, and now the sight of Austin has me in a tailspin.

Deep breath. I flatten my palms on my thighs and focus on breathing. I'm here. At the Olympics. It's not how I thought it would be, but I'm still here. Still had enough points to qualify on my own. It was only a run of bad luck that kept me off the team. So it's time to stop overthinking and second guessing. The thing with Austin doesn't need to be resolved now. There will be chances once the games are over. Trying to figure it all out here, even if he remembered what happened, would complicate race preparations, which is the only thing that should matter.

Okay. Yeah. That makes sense. I exhale slowly and slide my hands down my shins until they hit the floor. I feel better. It's not like we were going to spend these pre-competition days walking hand in hand through cute mountain villages and having sexy snowball fights that turned into hurried blow jobs in wintery woods. We're here to compete. Everything else is for later. That was always Austin's plan.

A knock on the door makes me jump. My hands shake as I reach for the knob. What if it's Austin? What will I say?

It's Ivan. His grizzled and permanently suntanned skin is unmistakeable, as is the faint sheen of silver along his jaw. Ski cross wasn't an official Olympic sport when he was competing. Instead, he won in the downhill, bringing home a gold medal in 1980. His racing and coaching career has lasted twice as long as I've been alive.

"Hi," I say.

"Good morning." His voice carries the gentle roll of early years spent in Ukraine before his family came to Canada while Ivan was still a kid. Technically, he could have competed for the Soviet Union, but in every news clipping from back then, he's always said Canada is his home. Still, he had to have made some hard decisions to get his career moving in a winning direction, and here I am acting like a doofus because I can't get my head out of my ass about a guy and a one-night stand we had months ago.

But Ivan has never been one for house calls, so if he's here at my door this early in the morning, something's up.

"Am I late for training?" I ask, though aside from a few more practice runs this afternoon, I'm pretty sure the official schedule is free for things like massage or physiotherapy. Can't overdo it on these last few days of training before the race.

He squints at me, like he's trying to read my mind. Sometimes I think he can. Ivan's coaching style has always been firm and serious. He's never mean and will tell you when you skied a shit race, but that's more out of a desire to see you do better than an instinct to shame.

"You have an appointment with Adiola," he says flatly.

My heart flutters in my chest. "Today?"

Adiola is the team psychologist. I don't see her very often. Or I didn't up until this year. She'll come in and give talks to all of us from time to time. Things like how to manage burnout. Using visualization techniques and how to cope with things like losing and injury. The things we all need to know. She also does periodic one-on-ones with team members, but in the past they were always pretty brief and informal. How have I been? Am I feeling stressed? What else am I doing in my life to keep skiing from being my only priority? The last question is always tricky, because skiing *is* my only priority. It's everyone's. We wouldn't be here otherwise. But somehow that always feels like the wrong answer when Adi asks it.

We've spent more time together this year, since my races were all such clusterfucks. The physical trainers gave me the all-clear, so obviously the issue was a mental one.

"This morning," Ivan says, tone still firm and making it clear he's not here to debate this. "After you finish breakfast."

So, like a bull stumbling through the proverbial china shop, I say, "I don't think I saw that on my schedule."

Ivan's gaze flashes, the only warning he ever gives before he puts his foot down. "It's on there now. Since yesterday, actually, when you decided to attack a teammate."

My mouth drops open. "What? I didn't attack anyone. Who would—" Then I remember smacking Austin with my pole. It wasn't exactly a full-on assault. Just some misdirected frustration. But Austin is the golden child, isn't he? The comeback king. And I'm the consolation prized shuttled in at the last minute due to someone else's screw-up. Of course I'm the one who gets to spend time with the psychologist. I clear my throat and square my shoulders before I face up to Ivan, but he cuts me off.

"I have tried to help you all season. If you can't conduct yourself like a professional on this hill, you don't get to race."

My anger shrinks back. He's not mad at me. He's never mad. Only disappointed. And he's right. Ivan's sat me down for so many one-on-one sessions this year. He knows there's a problem and tried his best to help, along with the rest of the coaching staff, but I would only ever talk about skiing with them. He even suggested I take some time off over the summer. Like real time. Lie on a beach. Maybe go out to BC and see Austin. But I insisted I was fine and ready to work, and he let the suggestion go. Not that I didn't see the look he gave me. The one that said he knew I was lying my ass off but he would treat me like an adult as long as I behaved like one.

That time is over. My behaviour yesterday wasn't very adult and he can scratch me from the race if he decides to. He's not here making polite suggestions or empty threats. This is not a negotiation.

"After breakfast," I say. He nods once, and then he's gone. My newly formed confidence and resolution go with him.

"SO HOW HAVE you been feeling since the last time we talked?" Adi asks, crossing one leg over the other. I'm used to talking to her online, and even the knowledge that she has legs is enough to throw me.

"Fine," I say, leaning back in my chair. We're in another hotel room, smaller than my shared one. "I mean, it's been a lot," I say, forcing a smile. "Four days ago I was home getting ready to watch the Olympics on TV and now I'm here."

She pushes away one of the braids that has fallen over her face. Adiola's originally from Guyana. She explained her background to me very clearly the first time we met. Two degrees from UofT in kinesiology and psychology, then graduate studies at McGill. I didn't really need her whole resume to be convinced she knows what she's doing, but I guess a lot of athletes do. We're so used to having every metric tracked and ranked to prove we've earned our spot, we want to know that everyone else has done the same too.

But since that first meeting, our relationship has become less formal. She's not big on things like jokes or smiling, but she listens, makes good suggestions, and isn't afraid to call me on my bullshit.

Like now, for example, where the silence hangs between us, and all she does is arch a single eyebrow to tell me she knows my little summary has left a lot of details out.

I sigh. "I'm tired. And wired. I thought I had missed my shot and now it's here and I don't want to blow it."

Adi nods, making notes. Like her legs, it's weird to be able to see her notebook. On a computer screen, every so often I will see her glancing down, and her shoulder moving like her hand is scribbling across a page. But getting the full 3D view now is as disorienting as everything else has been since I arrived in Italy.

"And your teammates?" she asks. "Have they made you feel welcome?"

Have they? What is she suggesting? That they should have rolled out the red carpet and baked me a cake?

"I guess," I say with a shrug. "I arrived late and everyone was scheduled for practice. Then my boot failed and . . ." More shrugging. This is so embarrassing. She's giving me that shrewd look like she knows I'm holding something back, and I feel like she's not going to let me leave until I tell her the truth. All of it.

"Austin looks good," I say, because maybe a compliment will save me from having to explain the whole pole-whacking thing yesterday.

Adi nods, making more notes. "This is the first time you've skied with him since he was injured, isn't it?"

She always says it like that. Since his injury. Since he was hurt. I always call it the accident. Talking about his injuries is too hard. Too scary. Too close to the even more terrible things that almost happened.

"How do you feel about him being here?" she asks.

"Great," I say, forcing my smile forward again. "I'm happy for him. His recovery has been incredible. Everyone's talking about it."

"Which means they're not talking about you," she says as she writes something down.

"What? No. I'm not jealous, if that's what you're saying." If anything, it's a relief to not be in the spotlight. I could be the story here. The sportscasters and commentators talking about my last-second qualification and what an uphill battle it's going to be for me to win here. If they'd rather talk about Austin and his recovery from basically being a pile of disassembled Lego pieces in a hospital bed, let them.

"I'm not saying anything," she says, in that infuriating therapist voice where she damn well is saying something but it's not the thing that she's *actually* saying. Subtext. Therapists love subtext. They love making you say the hard thing, then repeating it back to you without all the hedging and stammering it took for you to set the thing free from your brain in the first place.

"It's not jealousy," I insist. "If he wants to be the team poster boy, good for him. I don't care about that. I care about—" The admission gets stuck in my throat because while my feelings are surging ahead, my memory is still stuck on the mental image of Austin in that hospital room. Adi presses her lips together, waiting patiently. Fucking therapists. The only thing they like more than subtext is the value of a dramatic pause.

Well, tough shit. I look down at my hands. I can wait her out.

"You care about Austin," she says softly, and when I nod, she continues. "You both underwent a significant trauma last season. We've talked about this."

We have, but even now I'm still not sure I believe her. Sure, sitting in the snow holding him and panicking that no one would find us was scary. But Adi and I have been over that whole thing a million times. I walked out of that forest with nothing more than pins and needles in my foot from sitting too long. Austin's the one who needed months of rehab and his own separate training program to get his body working again. All I had to do was qualify for the Olympics in a sport I've spent my whole life training for, and I couldn't even do it.

Also, I've never told Adi about that night. It didn't seem right. Not that she'd tell anyone. Team gossip is more contagious than mono at a summer camp, but Adi's a professional.

But if I couldn't even bring myself to tell Austin it happened, there's no way I was going to tell a shrink. Besides, it's a completely separate thing. Sure, the accident was traumatic. The night before? Best night of my life. Why would I need therapy about that?

"I'm fine," I say for what feels like the tenth time since I walked into her makeshift office. The pause that follows is even heavier than the last. She knows I'm lying, but she can't force me to say anything. I used to worry that therapists had sneaky ways to pry uncomfortable truths out of you, but the real truth is I've never said anything to her I didn't want to. Case in point: she still thinks I'm hung up on Austin's accident and not the fact he said he loved me and promptly forgot about it.

She says, "I'm only here to help you compete as well as you can. If there's something standing in the way, we can talk about it."

I pinch my lips together because I'm not ready to say the thing she wants from me. Not now. It's too late now. I'm at the Olympics. There's no room to deal with broken hearts. If I was going to tell her about that, it should have been months ago.

As I leave our appointment, an arm slips into the crook of my elbow.

"There you are. I've been looking everywhere for you."

It's Tara the Terror. She smiles sweetly at me, but her grip on my arm says whatever is about to happen will be done her way. No delays from me. I'm used to competition weekends running on a tight schedule, but the Olympics are a whole new ballgame.

"What's up?" I ask.

"I need you and Austin on the bus in ten minutes. Can you do that?"

I can be on the bus in ten minutes. No problem. But with Austin?

"I'm not his keeper."

She arches an eyebrow in an expression that is annoyingly similar to one Adi gave me not too long ago. It leaves me feeling like I'm made of tissue paper and everyone can see right through me.

"I heard about your little thing yesterday at practice. We can't be having any of that in front of the cameras, hmmm?" The last sound curls up sweetly, but her fingernails on my sleeve are more like a cat about to strike.

"What cameras?"

Her grip tightens on my arm even further and I'm very close to getting scolded like a middle schooler in front of all the people who are now up and moving about. It's not only the Canadian freestyle team staying here either. Australians, Norwegians and Germans. Pretty sure I saw a couple people in what I think is the national team gear from Luxembourg. They're all moving through the central foyer of the hotel, carrying equipment and calling out to each other, but heads will turn when Tara starts yelling.

"It's on the schedule," she says instead, speaking through tight lips. Clearly she doesn't want to cause a scene either and for that I'm grateful. At least with Tara, whatever she's shuttling me and Austin off to, it's probably something media related. We'll smile and tell some journalist how excited we are to be here and that we're taking it one day at a time. No big deal. No emotional confessions. That's not what the world's sports broadcasters expect from us.

"I'll get my coat," I say.

Nine and a half minutes later, Austin and I are sitting as far apart from each other as possible inside the same ten-seater van Tara used to bring me up from the airport. He got on first, so sitting three rows back was my choice. Childish? Sure. But I'm still feeling a little raw from my chat with Adi, and anyway, the second the van door closes, Austin slumps to one side, squishing his team jacket under his head like a pillow. I let my chin drop and nap as best I can too.

Unfortunately, we don't go very far. Twenty minutes later, we're pulling up to the main lodge at the base of the mountain.

The driver rolls down his window and tells a man wearing a reflective vest something in Italian, and we're waved through.

"They're using the main lodge as the media centre for all the events at Livigno," Tara says. She pops her seatbelt off the second the van rolls to a stop. "Come on. We're late."

"Late for what?" I ask from the back of the van, because I still have no clue what we're doing. Austin shakes his head as he exits, but he doesn't say anything.

We follow after Tara as she takes us through the media centre. Ski lodges around the world all have a certain vibe. High ceilings. Carpet that's been trod on by decades of wet slushy ski boots, but is necessary to keep the people wearing those boots from slipping and killing themselves before they ever get on the hill. Tall windows that give you a view of the mountain. The faint smell of sweat from clothes that never fully dry between runs. Today, all of the usual tables and chairs where people would gather to eat or sip a hot chocolate to warm up on a cold day have been taken away, and tiny media stages have been set up side by side. Camera crews crouch, ready to record, as well-dressed journalists stand in front of green screens or sit behind desks, speaking in a crush of languages I don't know. I spot a few reporters I recognize from different events and start to drift to the left when I spot the set that's been erected for the Canada Sports Broadcast Network, because clearly that's where we're headed, right? But as I'm about to greet Pete Waterstone, Canada's favourite sports broadcaster, who is currently reading notes to himself behind a desk, Tara clicks her fingers and points to a door at the far end of an aisle between all the small sound stages. I duck my head, dropping my gaze like I've been caught doing something I shouldn't, and follow after her again.

She leads us outside, toward a separate area that looks like the kind of play space they use for little kids learning to ski. Lots of equipment in primary colours. Arches to ski under. The two official mascots for the games in tall cut-outs fixed into the snow.

Flags flutter in a soft breeze. And two people in CSBC-branded gear wave at us as we arrive.

"Hey guys!" the woman says. She looks like she's maybe a little older than me. Asian, with dark hair braided in pigtails.

"We're so glad you're here," the man behind her says. He's Black and maybe a couple years older too. He's got a tall, lean build like someone who goes to the gym for fun, rather than because it's his job.

We shake hands and introduce ourselves while Tara says, "This is Ray and Chantale from the CSBC content team."

Something shivers up my spine. Content team? That doesn't sound good. What happened to a quick interview with Pete about the honour of representing my country?

But Ray and Chantale clap their hands and look way too excited considering it's nearly minus fifteen degrees outside and we're not moving enough to stay warm.

"We're so excited you agreed to do this with us," Chantale says with a huge smile.

"Sure," Austin says. "It sounded like fun." But when he glances my way, his expression is nervous, not like he's pleased to be here.

"Uh, I'm sorry," I say, because admitting now I have no idea what's happening won't get me killed. Tara doesn't like to have witnesses. "What exactly did we agree to do?"

Chantale and Ray's grins get even wider and they laugh like my question is hilarious.

"It's part of CSBC's new digital media programming. We're going to play some games," Chantale says. "Come on! It'll be great!"

She waves her arm and she and Ray hurry off to the preschool play area, which maybe isn't set up for kids after all. Austin follows, but I stay where I am for a second. Games? What kind of games? And why me and Austin? Where's Kage? Matthieu? Surely Tara should have brought someone from the women's team along?

But she's not worried about any of that. Instead she puts her hands on my shoulders and turns me until I'm facing the table where Austin and the two super smiley twins are waiting for me. Then she gives me a shove.

"Play nice," she says, and the two words are not a request. They're a warning. I may not be having an intimate sit down with Pete Waterstone, but I'm still representing my country, and Tara will make sure I get buried in an avalanche if I screw this up.

Play nice. Sure. I can do that.

Right?

CHAPTER
FOURTEEN

WE GET FITTED out with microphones as Ray gives us the rundown for what's going to happen.

"So there's a few challenges," he says. "The first is a food challenge, the second is about how well you know each other, and if there's time, the third is a little race around our course here. Sound good?"

I nod. Austin claps his hands together, the sound muffled around his gloves. Along with the red-yellow-blue decor, the production crew has set up a few propane heaters, and once Austin and I are seated in front of a table, they wheel them just close enough that I can almost feel their warmth on one side of my face.

When the cameras start rolling, Chantale and Ray launch into a perky introduction before turning to me and Austin.

"Today we're here with Canadian ski cross athletes Austin Grimm and Cedric Berard. Welcome," Chantale says.

We nod and smile and say the right things about thank you for having us and how nice it is to be here, even though my toes are getting cold in my boots.

"You guys grew up together. You've been friends for a long time. What's it like to be here at the Olympics trying to beat each other for the gold medal?" Ray's eyes gleam as he asks his question. No doubt this is as close to "gotcha" journalism as a digital content team gets.

Austin looks towards me, gaze tentative, which makes my stomach sour. He shouldn't look at me like that, but also I'm the one who made him feel that way. Yesterday. Every day that I didn't text or call while he was working on getting better.

When our silence stretches a little too long and Tara, standing behind the cameras and looking tense, starts to strain up on her tiptoes, Austin says, "Going to the Olympics together has always been the plan. No one pushes me harder than Cedric does. All we can do while we're here is race our best and see what happens, but I'm glad I get to experience it with my best friend." As he finishes, his gaze settles on mine, and I grip the edges of my seat. My cheeks get so hot I don't even need the propane anymore.

"There was a time not that long ago that it wasn't even clear if Austin was going to make the Olympics after his injuries last season," Chantale continues. "Cedric, how do you feel about that?"

I have to swallow hard around the lump in my throat. Austin won't look away from me, so I'm the one who has to blink and lean forward so I can see past him at the two smiling reporters. I say, "He's one of the toughest people I know. If anyone could come back from that, it's Austin."

Their smiles get wider, pleased with the soundbites. Who cares if it's not true? Or is it? I chew on the inside of my bottom lip and fidget on my seat. Austin sounded sincere. This is the problem with hardly having talked for all these months. I don't know where his head is at. I'm so up inside my own head I hardly even know how to be around him, and the pressure cooker that is the last few days before the start of Olympic competition is the worst possible time to figure things out. I should have reached out more. Should have been braver.

But before I can say any of that out loud, we're moved on to the first segment of the show. Production assistants bring out trays covered with silver domes like we're at a fancy restaurant. Then they hand us each plain black blindfolds. I can't help myself when I glance at Austin. He's eyeing the whole thing with an expression that must make Ray and Chantale proud, like he's excited for whatever is about to happen.

"So the first challenge is about how well you know the countries competing at these games. On the plates are pieces of famous dishes from each of the participating countries. You're going to put the blindfolds on and feed each other parts of the food, and the other person will have to guess what country it's from." Chantale beams while Ray drums on the table. "Are you ready? Who wants to go first?"

I feel like I'm supposed to be somewhere else. Maybe back talking to Adi, or somewhere on the hill doing another walk through on the course. But instead, Austin and I give each other one more nervous glance. He shrugs. I say, "Sure. I'll go first," and slide the blindfold on because if my eyes are covered, I can't be looking at him and wondering how to get out of this hole I've dug for us, and possibly off this set without Tara hunting me down. In fact, the last thing I see before the world goes black is Tara glaring at me. Her expression dares me to do anything other than what I'm explicitly instructed to, and I give her what I hope is a reassuring little nod. I'll behave. This may not be quite the national television broadcast I might have expected, but it's still the CSBC. I'll be a good boy.

A soft clinking sound signals Austin lifting the dome off one of the plates. Somehow the space around us gets really quiet, apart from murmured commentary from our two hosts, who say things like "Oh, that looks really good" and "I think I had one of those last night." The absence of any visual cues means, without intending to, I lean forward, searching for more information on what's happening. I'm practically sniffing the air like a dog, then jolt back when something firm and smelling deep fried bumps against my lips.

"Hold still," Austin says, laughing softly.

Oh. That was his fingers. Are we really about to do this?

Slowly, I open my lips. Cold air rushes in, but then there's another whiff of the same fried thing again, before the morsel of food tumbles into my mouth. It's also cold . . . or at least not hot. Lukewarm at best, like it's been sitting outside for too long. Meat and maybe some fried dough. I chew, trying to sort out flavours.

"Come on," Austin says. "These are basically your favourite when we—"

"Shh," Chantale says, though her tone is joking. "No hints."

I chew some more. It's kind of bland, and the lack of warmth doesn't help. It would be better if it had like a sauce or something salty that—

"Oh. Gyoza," I say, finally swallowing. "From Japan." Chantale and Ray cheer like I've already won a gold medal. I sit up a little straighter, fighting down unearned pride. It's a silly video for social media. Austin sticking his fingers in my mouth will be a meme before we even—

The thought sends my pulse spiking at old memories of his fingers and more in my mouth. His skin under my tongue. Goddammit, why can't I have a single moment's peace around him?

"Okay, here comes the next one," Ray says, and before I can even prepare myself, Austin basically punches me in the mouth . . . even if it's gently.

"Hey," I say, jerking my heads back while the hosts laugh some more. Austin is laughing louder now.

"Sorry," he says. "Ready?"

This next offering is even blander than the first. Gyoza really are best with sauce, but at least the pan-fried bottoms give them some texture. This next food is basically like glue in my mouth. Just cold wrapping on the outside and something soft like mashed potato.

"Wait. Are these all dumplings?" I ask around my mouthful. The only reply I get is a conspiratorial "oooooh" from Ray and Chantale.

"Do you know what it is?" Austin asks.

"Is there any more?" It really didn't taste like anything.

"A little," Austin says, and this time I hold my mouth open, waiting. But instead of another soft mouthful, what I get is something cool against my bottom lip, followed by the tip of Austin's finger against my tongue. It's his turn to jerk away, leaving me with my mouth hanging wide in the cold air. "Sorry. There was a little bit of the—"

"No hints!" Chantale calls again, but she doesn't need to remind him, because I've already licked the sour cream off my bottom lip and that plus the potatoey flavour from before is all I need to know.

"Pierogi," I say. "From . . ." Shit. Where does pierogi come from? The freezer aisle at pretty much any grocery store at home, but I'm pretty sure the answer isn't Canada in this case. "Russia?" I ask, which leads to some cheerful but reproachful commentary, because apparently the answer is Poland, and while those two countries might be in the same part of the world, I'm sure Poland at least doesn't want to get confused for Russia and probably vice versa too.

"Okay, last one for Cedric!" Ray says, as I start to wonder exactly how long this segment is supposed to be. I don't have much time to spend on social media, especially not during the winter, but even I know attention spans aren't what they used to be and most people will have scrolled away before I was even done with the gyoza.

"No pressure, Zed," Austin says, and the sound of the old nickname from his lips has my face and body heating again. It doesn't quite reach my toes, but more than another undercooked piece of international cuisine, I want to hear him say it again. I missed him. Missed the closeness of him. "Three for three. You ready?"

The earnestness in his voice has me nodding hard. I want to please him. Make him proud. I want to undo whatever it is I've done between us. It doesn't matter if he remembers that night.

Doesn't even matter that he's probably not in love with me anymore. Not after the way I've been with him the last few months. But I've missed my friend so much.

"Open wide," Austin says and I do. Or I try to at least. But even with my best efforts, suddenly firm fingers grip my chin and pull it down, opening my mouth even wider, and I really hope the microphone pinned to my coat doesn't pick up the soft groan that escapes unchecked from my throat at his touch. But before I can panic about it, he slips something new into my mouth. It's bigger than the last two. Maybe the size of a marshmallow or a golf ball. Big enough that I have to quickly collect myself to keep from choking on it as it tries to slide down my throat unchewed. I clamp my teeth down on it to keep it in place and something explodes. Literally. One second, there's a dumpling of unknown origin in my mouth and the next it's gushing savoury goo in all directions. I don't even have time to close my mouth before it oozes out over my chin. I put my hand out to catch it, but the hilarious laughter from Ray and Chantale say I've failed. Without asking permission, I swipe the blindfold off. The two hosts are doubled over, giggling. Even Austin is watching me with a big, silly grin on his face. I glare at him as I work to contain and swallow his last offering, and don't move away when he picks up a paper napkin and wipes at my chin with it.

"What was that?" I ask, taking the napkin from him to clean up what looks like running brown gravy off the front of my Team Canada coat. Great. If this stains, I'll definitely win a medal and the world will get to witness my slobbery as I stand on the podium.

"You tell us," Chantale calls.

The plate in front of Austin is empty except for little crinkled papers like muffin wrappers and even smaller tent cards with tiny flags printed on them. The red circle for Japan. Red and white stripes for Poland. Red with yellow stars for China, so . . .

I chew again. Most of the dumpling is gone, but the goo clings to the inside of my cheeks.

"Soup dumpling," I say. "A really juicy one."

Everyone laughs, even Austin. His face crinkles up in joy, and it's such a relief after the last clear memory of him I have being the same face creasing with pain that something inside me loosens for the first time in months. He's okay, right? Has to be, if he can laugh hard enough most people would bust a rib, let alone someone who cracked several less than a year ago.

We do another round of food tasting, this time with Austin wearing the blindfold. Instead of more dumplings, I get a selection of noodles, which is even more impossible for Austin to eat cleanly than the soup dumpling was. No one offers me a fork or some gloves, so I wind up trying to tip the wrappers into his mouth.

"No, don't eat the paper, doofus," I say, as he excitedly chomps down on the first one. The warning has everyone laughing again, including Austin, which only helps to get what was supposed to be Swiss mountain macaroni and cheese dumped onto his lap. "Great," I sigh, muttering softly. "Now we're both going to have to dry clean our stuff before the medal ceremony."

"Ohh," Ray says, picking up on my words. "Does that mean you think you're both going to medal in ski cross? Who will come first?"

I bite down on my tongue. Traitor.

"Where's the food?" Austin asked, head bobbing like a baby bird.

"In your lap, dumbass," I say, then wonder if "dumbass" can be said on a national sports show, even one only destined for online spaces. Austin pats around his thighs, looking for his snack. I stare up at the sky, but if I can't say dumbass, there's no way I can be seen fondling his crotch to rescue some macaroni. My mom might see this. His too.

Finally, he gives up and we move on to jjajangmyeon from Korea, which I can barely pronounce and Austin certainly can't identify, then a third option with the Italian flag that might be spaghetti bolognese or something else entirely. I'm not really good at identifying my pastas. Austin isn't either. He guesses fettuccine, and Ray and Chantale take great pride in informing us its tagliatelle. We've probably just insulted the entire nation of Italy, so when Austin pulls off his blindfold, I mutter, "Sorry," and he smiles.

"Don't be sorry, Zed," he murmurs, but the way he holds my gaze says maybe my apology was for something else, and maybe he knows that too. I go back to staring at the sky while Ray and Chantale tally up the points and say we're moving on to something more physical. Good. My ass is falling asleep on the hard stool they gave me, and I can barely feel anything from my knees downward as the cold seeps farther up my limbs.

The other challenge turns out to be a sort of relay competition involving the cut-out mascots I noticed as we arrived.

"Dress them for a day on the slopes, bringing over one piece of equipment at a time. You can get more gear by answering questions so we can find out how well we know these two best friends. Sound good?" Ray asks, watching us expectantly, though what are we going to say?

"You ready?" Austin asks me.

I could tell him he's the one with cheese sauce on his crotch, which is so much worse than dumpling soup on my chest, but instead I shake my limbs like a fighter getting ready for the bell.

"You're going down, Grimm."

The concept is pretty much as simple as Ray described. Two tables are filled with a bunch of winter clothing. Toques, gloves, goggles, scarf. Two production assistants stand ready to pass one piece each, which we will then run up the slope to where the mascots stand, already wearing their illustrated Olympic wear, but I guess we're going to stretch the real thing over their heads and little paws.

The first question for each of us is the same. "What month is Cedric and Austin's birthdays?"

"October," I say, for which I am rewarded with a blue knit

toque. I take off at a run and over my shoulder, I hear Austin say, "October. No. September?"

"You don't even know when my birthday is?" I call.

"I wanted to give you a head start." His feet crunch on the snow, but I'm already halfway to my mascot. I'm not sure the little furry creature can see properly once I slap the hat over his head, but no one said he needed to be able to do anything once he was dressed.

The return trip is tricky. It's not exactly a steep pitch, but it drops enough to make it treacherous in the snow. I have to shuffle to keep from crashing into the PA as Ray reads my next question.

"In what country did Austin win his first World Cup event?"

"France," I say without a second thought, holding my hands out for the goggles.

"Wrong!" Austin says, skidding to a stop beside me.

"What?" I ask, because I remember his win clearly, but Ray also shakes his head and asks the question again.

"If Cedric weren't on the national team, what would he do for work?" Chantale asks Austin.

"Trick question!" Austin says confidently. "He has no backup plan. He says it keeps him competitive." He snatches up the goggles and runs.

I shake my head, trying to focus, thinking back to that first win. It was in France, two years ago. We were there with Matthieu and he took us to a—

"No!" I say. "It was in Switzerland." Talk about a trick question. Officially, the town we stayed in was in France, but the resort was massive and the part where we competed was actually on the Swiss side of the Alps.

Ray smiles and hands me the goggles. Austin is already fumbling with his mascot, trying to get the goggles to stay on over the flimsy cardboard. He's running back before I'm even halfway to mine.

"Gotta pick it up, Zed," he calls as we pass, so close we nearly brush shoulders. I'm breathing hard and the chill in my legs and feet has disappeared. My blood is pumping and the thrill of competition—even ridiculous family-friendly social media competition—has my focus sharpening with every step. Just because I'm behind now doesn't mean I'm out of it. Races can always change.

"What is Cedric's favourite way to stay active in the off-season?" Chantale asks.

"Oh, that's too easy!" I call as I turn to run back.

"Mountain biking." Austin says, taking one of the gloves offered by the PA.

I need a backup plan. If they're going to softball him like that, I'll never win. Without really thinking about it, I rush to Austin's mascot, ripping the hat and goggles from its head and throwing them into the snow.

"Hey!" Austin calls. "No cheating."

"It's not cheating," I say as my feet slip in the downhill rush. "No one said anything about not interfering with the other person's mascot."

"It's true," Ray says, laughing. No doubt they didn't even think about it, but if it makes good content, they're going to run with it.

As I go to pass Austin on my return, for a second it looks like he trips. I slow, because no way can he get hurt in this ridiculous game days before competition, but as I do, he pops up again, hands full of fluffy snow, which he throws in my face.

"Dude," I say, laughing. Snow slides under the collar of my coat, burning against my skin. I'm so caught up in trying to get it out, I don't see Austin running for me until it's too late. His arms wrap around me and he tackles me to the ground. The snow cushions the impact, but there's still an entire man sprawled on top of me.

"Get off," I say, but I'm laughing. No idea if the microphone will pick it up, or if Austin's jacket bunched up against mine will block the sound. I squirm, rolling us towards the side of the area where the snow is even deeper.

"No. No, no!" Austin's laughter rings out in the cold. I make sure to stuff a few handfuls of snow into his coat for good measure. He grabs hold of my wrist, trying to stop me, and we freeze, staring at each other. Somewhere close by, the shutter of a professional-grade camera clicks, but I only have eyes for Austin. His gaze is clear, cheeks pink and, even in all his outerwear, suddenly I'm back in bed with him, all those months ago, watching his open expression as he promises me forever. His breath puffs up towards me in little clouds from the cold, and his lips part, like he's about to say something we definitely don't want the masses to hear.

I vault back up to my feet, taking him with me as I brush the snow off his coat. His expression clouds, and he doesn't return the favour, which leaves me to shake the snow away on my own.

Chantale and Ray are standing by the tables with their remaining ski gear, but the glance they give each other is uneasy. I check Austin again, but he's watching something off to his left and clears his throat.

"We'll call it a tie!" I shout with a smile. The two hosts nod eagerly.

"The two of you certainly have some . . ." Chantale pauses, like she can't quite think of the right word. "Chemistry."

Yeah. We do. We did. Austin knows me better than anyone else in the world, even the parts he's forgotten.

"Do you have all the footage you need?" Tara asks, glancing up from her phone. "I have to get them back for practice."

We film a quick wrap-up where the hosts thank us for playing and wish us luck. Just like our arrival, Austin and I don't talk as Tara leads us back through the media centre and toward the waiting van. The air between us has changed and when I get into the van first, Austin follows me, so that I have no choice but to let him sit next to me when he joins me in the back row.

"You okay?" he asks as we pull out of the parking lot.

"Of course," I say, though my reassuring smile feels stiff on my face. "You're lucky you chose ski cross. You'd have never made it in football."

He laughs softly, pulling his black and red Canada-branded toque off to scratch at his head.

"Are you okay?" I ask and the question feels heavy on my tongue.

His smile turns wry. "Why wouldn't I be? I tackled you, remember?"

I shrug, feeling uncomfortable. "I wasn't sure if . . . with everything. I wasn't sure if you could—"

"Take a hard landing?" he asks, and I nod. Even after all this time, even after today and his easy laughter as we ran back and forth, I can't believe he's okay. He was so broken that night in the hospital. How can anyone ever be okay after that? But Austin shrugs and says, "Yeah, I'm fine. They wouldn't have let me come if I wasn't a hundred percent."

Up at the front of the van, Tara says, "Ivan wants you ready to be on the mountain in thirty minutes, okay?" And the question breaks the quiet bubble that Austin and I have been building. We both acknowledge the question that isn't really a question, then sit in silence all the way back to the resort.

The million and one things I want to say stay trapped inside my chest. But maybe they won't stay there much longer.

CHAPTER
FIFTEEN

AFTERNOON PRACTICE GOES BETTER. Which isn't to say it goes well, but at least I don't fall on my face. With so little time left before competition, we aren't here to push ourselves. Everyone wants to be in peak shape for the first seeding heat and the eliminations that follow. No need to risk serious injury by doing runs at top speed now. Instead, we go through individual sections of the course, taking the turns slowly, then riding snowmobiles back to the top of the curve to do it all over again. By the end of the day, I'll be able to visualize the whole run while standing still with my eyes closed. Or I should be able to. I've done it many times before. Somehow today, each approach to the turn feels like an entirely new trail. I find new dips and previously unexpected places where the ground drops away. No matter how many times we do it, I still feel like I'm learning it all over again.

"Berard, get your head out of your ass," Ivan growls, proving my point.

At least I'm not alone. If I'm struggling to find a consistent line, Austin is failing. This time it's him who wipes out as we work through the initial hurdles of the start sequence. I try not to look back to see if he's okay. He said he could take an impact, and it's not like I can look for him or anyone else if they fall in an actual race. Someone's fall is my gain, after all. But when I hear Austin's muffled *oof*, it's everything I can do not to spread my skis out to slow and check on him.

"Grimm, you okay?" Ivan calls, because of course Austin gets the kid glove treatment. Nice to know I'm not the only one worried about him, at least.

But the challenges he has today hold me back too. Every time he falls behind, or I hear him slip a little too far off the ideal line, grinding his edges into the hard surface of the snow, I tense, waiting for the sound of his body hitting the ground.

Just like it did during that ridiculous relay race. Tackling me like that was a huge risk for Austin. How does he know he's okay? Even the doctors are guessing at best. They're assuming, but they don't know for sure.

Distracted by nightmare scenarios of Austin lying bleeding in the snow, I catch an edge and, even though I'm not going very fast, tumble into the bank of the turn, jamming my shoulder.

"Ow. Shit."

"Third place is first loser!" Kage calls as he slides past me.

"Okay?" Austin asks, stopping just below me.

I scoff. "Why wouldn't I be?"

"You fell."

His attention makes me uncomfortable. I pick at the snow with one of my pole baskets. "That was hardly a fall. I'm not made of glass."

"Neither am I," he says, making my pole skitter on the ground. "Don't treat me like I am."

I look up at him. He's standing with his back to the sun, and the light in the dry winter air makes a halo effect, punctuated by sparkling flecks of snow that float lazily around him. He looks like an angel, and I have to shake my head, because now is not the time to get all sappy about my best friend. Not when things are finally starting to feel normal. All I need to do is focus on getting through the next few days skiing the best I can. Yesterday won't win me a medal. Not that mindset and not that lack of focus. If Austin wants to be okay, I have to take him at his word and concentrate on skiing my race.

"No problem," I say, pushing up to my feet.

The others are farther along the run. Austin stops with his methodical exploration of the course and instead points his skis downhill. I do the same. He doesn't even have to look at me. Just his posture tells me what's coming. He pushes off, arms, thighs and feet working to get him moving as fast as possible, and I follow. He's slightly ahead of me, aiming for the midline of the turn. If I duck under him, I can take the shorter path and—

We rocket off the turn side by side. My body is crouched, trying to make myself as small as possible on the flats. When we hit the next jump, I hear a soft grunt from him as we're launched into the silence of open air while the mountain drops away for one . . . two . . .

Wh-whap.

Shit. Austin hits the snow a split second before I do, and that's all he needs to press his advantage. He tucks in, skis parallel and aiming directly for the next turn, where Ivan, Matthieu, and Kage are waiting on the side of the trail. We shoot past them, moving too fast to even hear what they say. I'm a half ski-length behind Austin, but I won't let him get away. The next section is a fast chicane with gates marking the path we have to take. Each turn pushes us to the brink of control, and with every second, Austin inches further ahead. The force needed to hold onto the snow here is extreme, like some invisible monster is trying to push me off course the whole time. My thighs scream as they bounce up and down in a rapid staccato like shock absorbers. Austin's fully in front now and he shouts. It's a loud, joyous sound. Relief. Delight. Slick tears stream from the corners of my eyes, and I tell myself it's the cold and the wind.

As we come over the last ridge, the world drops away one

more time. I've closed the gap so my boots are in line with the backs of his skis. If I can hit the snow before he does, I might have a chance to—

Whap.

We come down at nearly the same time, but he's still faster. The bottom of the race is in view. Nothing now but to head straight for the ending. His form is perfect, and I find myself forgetting about passing him because the view from here is spectacular. Strong back and legs. Shoulders tucked in and his arms framing his torso. He's a bullet. As good as I ever remember. How could I have thought he'd be anything less, even after everything that happened?

Austin slides over the finish line two lengths ahead of me and holds his arms up in conquest like he's actually won something. When he glances back at me, his victory now secured, his smile is playful. There's no pain. No fear. He's the same person he's always been. The one from before the accident, who cracked jokes and dreamed big with me. It's only the mass of team and race officials, trainers, and athletes that keeps me from flinging myself into his arms when I finish our improvised race. Who cares our skis would get in the way? That we'd inevitably wind up in a tangle of limbs on the cold, hard ground? That one of us would probably tear something less than forty-eight hours before go time? He's here. Austin is here. I only had to look for him behind all my own hang-ups and trauma.

Maybe all that therapy with Adi actually is working.

Instead, I slide to a stop behind him, bending at the waist and supporting myself on my poles as I breathe hard.

"Gonna have to ski faster than that if you want to win," Austin says, eyes crinkling at the corner as he smiles so hard his face might break.

"I was going easy on you. Wanted to boost your confidence. Comeback kid and all that." But my bravado gets undermined by my heavy breathing. I was much closer to giving that everything I had than I'd ever admit, and Austin looks like he was out for a five-kilometre fun run on a sunny morning.

He laughs at my display, then pushes off. He sways from side to side as he skates over the snow, headed toward the lift.

"Come on. Ivan will be pissed."

Worth it. No amount of preparation and talking through the course was going to fix what was going on inside my head. It was never a strength and strategy problem.

When we slide onto the lift, I let out a long exhale. The kind I've been holding in the very bottom of my lungs for months, maybe longer. Austin pulls the safety bar down over our heads, leaning against it, face pointed up to the thin winter sun. His eyes are closed and his mouth is turned up in the corners, making the gentlest smile.

"That was really fun," he says, and the relaxed ease in his voice pours over me like warm honey.

"The winner always thinks racing is fun," I grumble, but I don't have any heat to put behind it. I'm not actually sore about losing. Getting to watch him ski like that was incredible. I have lots more days to beat him, along with the thirty other athletes who will try to take my place at the top of the podium. Today isn't about that.

"Oh my god," he says with a happy groan, leaning back. "You should have seen my first day back on skis. You'd have laughed so hard. My legs were like noodles. No strength in them whatsoever."

The light feeling in my chest sinks. I don't want to think about that. All the months. The work. The pain. I only want to think about now. The after, when he's okay and everything can be like it was before.

Austin opens his eyes and looks at me. His smile fades.
"What?"

I shake my head, pressing my lips together tight to keep from saying all the things that are trying to get out at once. The chair is wide, made to seat four skiers across and we're alone, but

Austin shimmies over until he's close enough to bump my shoulder.

"What is it?" he asks, and now his voice has gone soft and serious, and the care I hear breaks me. I look away, staring out over the snow reflecting bright in the sunshine. It makes me squint as I wipe a gloved hand awkwardly at the corners of my eyes. No wind to hide my tears this time. Austin bumps me again, leaning into me. "Hey. What's wrong?"

I shake some more. My head. My whole body. If I start talking, I might never stop, and this ride on the chair will end soon enough.

He threads an arm through mine, the material of our coats swishing against each other. Austin rests his head on my shoulder, or at least he tries to. Our helmets bang together with an empty *thunk* that has me wondering if there's anything inside our heads to protect. Not in mine, that's for sure. I got so worked up over seeing him. Speaking with him. Just being around him. I nearly killed our friendship and my chance to reach the goals we set for ourselves when we were only kids dreaming big.

The chairlift comes to a sudden halt, swaying on the heavy cable overhead.

"Oops," I say. It's not uncommon for lifts to stop. A staff person traveling to the top of the hill needs extra time to unload gear, or a newbie misjudges the procedure and falls . . . or stays on too long and has to be rescued.

Except there aren't too many newbies around. This whole mountain is closed to non-athletes. Could be staff then. Someone bringing an extra pair of skis up, or ski patrol carrying a sled, just in case . . . though more often than not in a big place like this and when high-speed crashes mean every second counts for a response, they'll travel by snowmobile with the sled hitched to the back.

The world falls silent and we stay perfectly still. There's no danger. There are urban legends and freak accidents where lifts and gondolas detach from the cable and fall, but most are myths, and the few that do happen are pretty rare. I slap my hands together, the impact pumping blood at my wrists and arms, trying to keep warm. The chair ahead of us is empty, as is the one behind.

"Zed," Austin says softly, and something about the sound of my name makes all the hair on my neck stand up on end.

"Yeah?" I ask. It's only a few letters, but my voice wobbles on every one and I blush. Watch him tell me he has to pee. Or that the energy bar he ate while waiting for our practice session isn't sitting well.

But instead he says, "I need to tell you something. I *want* to tell you something. I was going to wait until after the games, but then . . ." He bounces a fist off the safety bar and when he glances at me, his cheeks are flushed and his eyes shine.

Oh god. He's going to say it. Again. Except he thinks it's for the first time. That this is going to be some surprise revelation. And what am I supposed to do? Be surprised? Shocked? Pretend like it was always going to be that way?

I don't want that. I don't want to be friends. I want the man who fumbled and laughed and promised me forever. And if he says it, he'll think that's what he's giving me, and he'll never know that we've already been forever to each other before.

Because I spent months hiding from him. I was scared. For him. Maybe a little scared of him. Of who I would have to be for him if I told him what had happened. That was selfish and I'm sorry. I'll tell him how sorry, once he knows. Because I'm not going to lie to him. Not going to hide anymore.

His lips are moving, like he's speaking, but nothing comes out. Austin plucks at one of the fingers on his glove, still looking nervous. I put a hand on his, squeezing reassuringly as I force myself to smile confidently and keep my voice steady.

"It's okay," I say. "I already know."

His eyes go round. For a minute, he looks like the kid I met on the mountain all those years ago. Big eyes and a round helmet.

"You . . . you do?" he stammers.

I could pretend I'm psychic. Tell him we're best friends with no secrets.

But I've kept so many secrets. And that ends now.

"I do," I say slowly. "Because you told me the night before your accident. You said you were in love with me. Austin, I've known for months."

CHAPTER
SIXTEEN

NOW WOULD BE A REALLY good time for the chairlift to start moving again. Austin is staring at me like he's never met me before. Or like I'm speaking in a foreign language.

"Did you hear me?" I ask, voice strained. "I said—"

"I heard what you said." He works his bottom lip between his teeth. It's a nervous gesture. "I . . . I told you?"

The question is heartbreaking, just like his face. I shouldn't have said anything. Would it have mattered if I'd gone along with his confession a second time? The ending would be the same, wouldn't it?

Only not really. He may not remember, but I do, and I can't pretend.

The chair shifts as he scoots farther away again, creating space between us. I let him have it. There was a while this summer where I convinced myself his amnesia or trauma or whatever this is was all an act. That one of these days he was going to text or call and let something slip or go "Surprise!" then reveal that he'd remembered everything, the same way I still do. But he never did, and that sort of thing probably only happens in movies anyway.

"I was going to tell you," Austin says finally. He sounds like he might cry.

"After the games. I know. You said that too."

He blinks a few more times, then goes back to picking at his gloved fingertips.

"Is that why you've been . . . the way you've been?"

Ugh, that's a complicated question. "Partly. Sort of. There's a lot. Adi and I have talked about—"

"You've been seeing the psychologist?"

"Yeah? Haven't you? You went through some major shit." I want to wrap my arms around myself protectively. Haven't we all been through some shit? That's what Adi says. If they made me talk to her and he didn't have to, I will be pissed.

On the slope below, a ski patrol is snow plowing his way down the mountain, stopping to shout something at the people in the chair a couple ahead of ours. They shout back and he slides down to us. His words are loud but unclear.

"What?" I ask, leaning over the bar and cupping a hand to my ear, even though that won't help, since when he repeats himself, it's clear he's speaking in Italian.

"No," I say, shaking my head. "English. Canada."

He pauses, hands planted impatiently on his hips. "There is no electricity," he says. "We fix. You wait."

As though we were doing anything else? But he doesn't stick around for an answer, only continues on down the hill toward the next occupied chair.

"Well, that's just great," I say, slumping back in my seat. If the power's out, we could be here a very long time. Like, hours. It's getting cold up here.

I'm about to crack a joke about huddling for warmth. Since the genie's out of the bottle—or the cat's out of the bag—surely Austin won't mind . . .

Shit.

I haven't told him everything, and if he doesn't remember saying he loves me, then what comes next might be an even bigger shock.

"How are you feeling?" I ask carefully.

He's still studying me like I could grow tentacles or scales at any moment, but eventually he shrugs. "Fine, I guess. A little cold. If they don't get the power back on—"

"No, I mean, do you have any lingering conditions I should know about? From the accident. High blood pressure? Brain bleed? Anything that means you shouldn't receive stressful news unprepared?"

He rolls his eyes. "You're being dramatic, Zed."

"I'm being serious. Are you okay?"

He makes a fist and rolls it around on his wrist. "This hurts when it rains. Sometimes the muscles between my ribs ache if I laugh too hard or sneeze funny. My ears get this ringing sound when it's really cold that the doctor says might be left over from the jaw fracture, but no one can say for sure."

My stomach rolls as the remembered sight of him lying in a crumpled heap of snow and blood replays itself in my memory. I have no idea how that broken person and the man in front of me are the same one.

"I was really scared," I say. "You were so hurt and I didn't know what to do."

It's not the confession I plan to make. I was going to tell him about the competition-worthy sex the night before. About the sound he made as I pushed my dick into him for the first time. About the embarrassing way I came all over myself as he played with my balls and licked my taint. About how I haven't been with anyone else since that night because no one would ever, *ever* be like he was, and as a horny twenty-three-year-old in his sexual prime, that level of restraint is extraordinary. There were opportunities, and I walked away from every single one of them because nothing would ever compare to him.

He shakes his head. "I don't remember."

"I know!" My voice comes out louder than I mean to and I bury my head in my hands. "You were going to die and there was nothing I could do but hold you and beg you to keep breathing.

And you don't even remember. You know what?" I round on him. "That's fine. Because I do. Every single time I close my eyes, it's all I can see. And you got to walk away."

"Walk away?" His eyes go wide. "I could barely walk at all. I was moving like an old man. Everything hurt all the time. You were scared? I didn't think I'd ever be okay again. That I would be in pain for the rest of my life. You think I can forget that?"

Our voices echo off the snow. His expression is furious. I don't care.

"You don't remember. You don't remember!" I say over and over.

It's not fair. It's not fair that we're this way. I don't know which is worse. That I remember all of it. Every single goddamn second. Or that he remembers none of it. The bad parts. The fear and the pain. But also the good too. Because there was so much good before, and for him, it's all gone, leaving me alone with all the memories.

He slides a little closer to me. Not so much that we can touch, but the gulf between us gets smaller. His closeness makes me flinch, but he doesn't back away.

He says, "They told me you came to see me in the hospital. The night of the accident."

I'm shaking as too many feelings war inside me. Did he feel better knowing I was there? Does he think I'm pathetic for needing to see him? Is it wrong that I'm mad that he wasn't there for me? He was rebuilding his body. Recovering. I know that. But he was gone in every single way that mattered, and I needed my friend. How am I supposed to tell him that?

All those months talking in therapy and suddenly I don't know what to say.

Austin comes even closer, so he can put one arm around mine. The pressure of his squeeze helps a bit.

"I don't even remember that," he says, *thunk*ing our helmets together again. "But I'm really glad you came. I needed you."

It's a nice thought. For him. I still don't feel better. He doesn't get to win. He doesn't get the last word.

"We had sex," I blurt. The truth falls out of me like vomit after a night of binge drinking. "Holy shit. We had sex. The night before the accident."

Another *thunk* as he retreats again quickly.

"What?" His face has lost its sweet pink shine and he's gone completely pale. His obvious shock makes me feel better. A little at least.

But I still can't stop. "So much sex. We kissed outside a bar and you said you loved me. We went back to the hotel and things were a little weird, until they weren't and then we fucked." I take a deep inhale. "Holy fuck, did we fuck. Like, for hours. All night. Doggy style. You on top. You sucked me off and I ate your ass and—"

"What?" He's got one hand on the chair's upright and the other on his chest and for a minute I think he might actually pass out. I envision him slithering from the chair and tumbling through open space and I can't even begin to think how I'd explain that to the ski patrol. Or what I'd say to the media when the story gets out and the people ask how Austin Grimm survived a horrible accident that shattered bones throughout his body and came back from it in time to achieve his Olympic dream, only to mysteriously plummet off a stationary ski lift and die and— "You ate my ass?"

The mountain falls silent again. My ears ring. Austin continues to stare at me. I could blow a puff of breath in his direction and he really would float away in the wind.

My bottom lip quivers and for a second I think I'm going to cry. Then I realize it's not tears I'm holding back. It's laughter. The shocked look on his face. The way his mouth hangs open after he finishes his question. A breeze brushes over us and makes a hollow whistling sound in the space between his lips, and that's what finally makes me lose it. The laughter bursts from me in a flurry of spit and hysteria. I laugh so hard a crow takes flight from a tall, skinny tree not far from us. Austin continues to watch me as expressions of stunned awe wash over his face. Every time I think I'm ready to pull myself together and answer his question, I look at him and start laughing all over again, until once more tears are pouring down my face. My cheeks hurt, and my stomach too, which makes me think of his ribs hurting when he sneezes and somehow that also seems funny now, and the giggling continues.

By the time I'm done, he's starting to look more than a little hurt. He's closed his mouth, but now he's pushing out his bottom lip in a pout that makes me want to kiss him. He's mine. My best friend. Brother on the snow. And I've told him now and he didn't freak out or run away . . . though right now, where would he go?

"I'm sorry," I gasp, wiping my eyes. "I didn't think it was going to come out like that."

"Like what?" He's still pouting. "You admitting you had your tongue in my ass ten months ago and never bothered to remind me that was a thing that happened?"

"Jesus." I glance backward at the people in the chair beyond the empty one. Austin's voice is rising loud enough they might be able to hear us. I don't recognize them, though. All I can hope is they don't speak English, or if they do, that they only understand the basics and will assume they've misheard. "You're the one who randomly told me you were in love with me ten months ago. Keep your voice down."

"Keep my voice down?" He's breathing hard again, but the colour is back in his cheeks at least. "*My* voice? Keep my voice *down*? After what you just said? You tell me that we f—"

I lunge for him, slapping a glove over his mouth to smother the words. We don't need the entire Olympic village hearing our business. Austin struggles against my hold for a minute, but then seems to realize at the exact same moment I do that we're suddenly very close. It's like us wrestling in the snow all over again. His breaths puff out of his nose, gusting over my hand, and his eyes sparkle with something like rage. A warning.

Need.

Holy shit. The last time I saw that look on his face, he pushed me down onto the bed and sucked my dick so far back into his throat I could see the entire fabric of the universe for a minute.

Very slowly . . . *so slowly,* I pull my hand away from his mouth. His lips are parted and he stays completely frozen in place. He's like a mannequin forgotten at the back of the warehouse, staring blankly into space. Searching the damaged remnants of his memory for any hint of what I'm saying? Trying to ward off the kind of erection that drains so much blood from the rest of your body that your fingers and toes start to tingle from lack of circulation? It's certainly what I'm doing right now.

"Well, what the fuck!" he shouts, and the same crow takes flight again, leaving the tree it sought refuge in after my first interruption. "I've spent all this time trying to figure out what I did wrong that you've been treating me like a parasite the whole time I was in BC, and meanwhile you get to replay a highlight reel of us fucking and—"

"Would you shut up?" I ask. I know this is a lot. He's trying to take it all in. But on the off chance anyone on this mountain speaks English—because at this point they can all hear him—I'd rather this story not get out.

The chair lurches into motion. Great. Austin keeps shaking his head. Maybe in disbelief but also like he's trying to dislodge something from his ear. See? This is why I asked about his physical condition. How do I know he's not slowly bleeding from his ears inside his helmet as he tries to come to grips with the revelation that we—

"I'm sorry," I say, mostly to get him to look at me, so I know he's okay. "I should have told you sooner."

"Yeah," he says, mouth set in a grim line. "You should have." But the line gets a little crooked. "Only not too soon. Those first couple weeks are all blurred together. Morphine is amazing, but for a while I thought my dad was my boyfriend and my mom was my high school geography teacher trying to break us up."

I roll my eyes. "Mrs. Callaghan always was a bitch like that."

He laughs. It's an old sound. Familiar. The laugh I've known my whole life but haven't heard since that night in the hotel room, tangled in sweaty, come-scented sheets.

We're okay. We're going to be okay.

CHAPTER
SEVENTEEN

WHEN WE REJOIN THE TEAM, we get a few looks from Matthieu and Kage. Raised eyebrows and half-hidden smiles.

"You two speaking again?" Kage asks, laughing when Matthieu jabs him with an elbow.

"So nice of you to come back to your training session," Ivan growls. "Unless you feel you don't need it two days before your Olympic debut?"

I go to protest about the delay with the lift, but Ivan's not really looking for explanations or excuses. Instead, we murmur apologies, promising to behave. And we do our best, though it's hard to stay focused. Austin knows. He may not remember, but he knows what happened. It's like the day of the shoot all over again, being so close I can touch him, but not being able to. Or at least not in the way I want. Now that it's out in the open, I want to climb inside his jacket. Breathe in his scent. Once again drag him off into the woods and see if it's possible to get through all his layers of clothes to give him the blow job he deserves after everything.

"Berard!" Ivan snaps. "Listen up."

I start, realizing I've been staring at Austin like a lovesick puppy. Kage is smirking. Matthieu rolls his eyes. Even Austin is blushing and clears his throat uncomfortably. I am so not even being subtle at this point. There might as well be hearts tumbling from my eyes and little birdies bringing me flower crowns. Who knew telling the truth would feel this good?

But I square my shoulders and nod, recommitting to paying attention. I have a lifetime to make Austin remember how good it feels to be in love with me. I have forty-eight hours to get my shit together and win a gold medal.

When our practice is over, I practically throw my skis into the gear tent. Well, not really. I'm not an asshole, and the equipment team has enough going on. But I drop them off as fast as I can, then rip my gloves from my hands.

"Come on," I say, pulling at Austin's arm as he drops his stuff off too.

"Where? We've got physiotherapy."

"I have a better idea for therapy. Still physical. And a team sport too. It'll be good for both of us." I leer. I don't actually know how to leer, but I think I do an okay job.

He smiles but digs in his heels, which is especially effective in his ski boots.

"But physio."

I pout. "Really?"

He rolls his wrist the same way he did on the lift, then moves his jaw back and forth like he's trying to relieve pressure in his ears.

"They get mad when I'm late," he says.

So he'll play the delicate card when it's convenient? Pain in my ass.

"Fine." But I pull him behind a fluttering tent flap. He laughs, but doesn't resist. I want to kiss him. Just once, to remind myself what it's like and—

Our lips are millimetres away when I pause.

"What's wrong?" he asks.

"This is your first kiss," I say.

Austin steps toward me, closing the final spaces between us, until all that separates us are the layers of clothes and outerwear we were silly enough to think we'd need today.

"I'm not a virgin," he says. His lips brush over mine as he speaks, but he doesn't stay still long enough to seal the deal.

My body is on alert, rising to the occasion, even if there's nothing we can do here.

"Oh, I'm very aware of that. Even more than you might be, given only one of us remembers the things we did together, but . . ." I brush a thumb against his mouth, feeling the soft but dry skin there. A stray fleck comes off under my touch, and he traces the path I took with the tip of his tongue. The small gesture makes me groan. "But it's the first kiss with me you're going to remember."

I expect him to tell me not to be so sentimental. Or to reassure me it doesn't matter. Instead, before I can even think of anything else to say, his mouth crashes down on mine. It's like outside the karaoke bar all over again. He sucks the breath from my lungs, and I have to grip his jacket to keep from falling backwards into the tent. He's rough and confident, sending me a silent reminder he really isn't breakable. I nearly fall anyway, because I try to rise up on my toes, to kiss him more . . . better . . . all of him, but ski boots really aren't made for this kind of thing, and only his hand on the small of my back keeps me from tumbling and taking him with me.

Finally, he pulls back, letting us both gasp. I settle more firmly on my feet. My cock is already half awake, pushing against my clothes.

"Physio," Austin says firmly, stepping away. "Team building later."

I whine. That's so not fair. But I follow after him, keeping my head down, in case anyone saw us.

Physio is torture. And not only because the therapist kicks my ass. Sure, he has me twisting and bending in positions that make everything in my body strain. There's weird tension in my left knee that wasn't there yesterday. Tightness that runs up my thighs and pulls at my ankle. Working it out is not fun, but nothing I haven't dealt with before.

What I haven't dealt with before is Austin and the team of therapists that descend on him when we walk into the treatment room. Usually treatment is done individually and privately, but given the volume of people to work on and the limited space of the hotel, the Canadian staff have set up a large common area with dividers between stations. I can't see Austin, but I can hear as his team ask a barrage of questions about his condition, his body, what hurts, and where he feels weaknesses. He gives direct answers like this is a ritual he has undergone many, *many* times in the months since he finally left the hospital.

Then he moans.

Okay, it's not immediately after he answers all those questions. I'm lying on a table with one of my knees bent against my chest, and he lets out a long, low groan. It's a deep "ohhhh" from the direction of his team, and my whole body goes tense.

"What was that?" Felix, the therapist I'm working with, asks. "Pain?"

If he only knew.

"No, it's okay," I say, focusing on breathing. But then Austin does it again as Felix releases me. I stare at the ceiling, listening to soft voices and the sound of Austin's evolving discomfort and relief. It's obscene, even if it's perfectly innocent.

"Other side?" Felix prompts me. I make up a mumbled excuse as I spin around so my head is at the other end of the table, which means when we stretch out this side, I'm still facing away. Even with the divider, there's no way I can face that direction with what's coming from beyond it. If I did, I'm going to embarrass myself very quickly. Hard-ons happen from time to time in sessions like this. You can't have someone this close to you, touching you and generating that sweet pleasure-pain of muscles releasing without sometimes it going other places in your head. But everyone's discreet about it, and honestly, as soon as the therapist is done, the feeling goes away, so things have never gotten too awkward for me.

But having Austin in the same room, making sounds like that . . . I'm only a man after all, and I know how to get him to make those noises when it's only the two of us. Like the sound he makes as I push his legs back and—

"Jesus Christ." I pop up to sitting like I've been electrocuted. Felix takes a surprised step back.

"You okay?" Austin asks beyond the divider.

I grip the edge of the table. "Yeah. I'll be right back." Without further explanation, I hop off the table and rush out of the room.

At this rate, I'm not going to make it to the podium. I may not make it to the end of today.

I'm waiting for Austin when he comes out of the therapy room. It's located on the second floor of the hotel, and that's still too far from my bed.

"You sure you're okay?" he asks, genuinely worried.

Not in the slightest. Unencumbered by heavy outerwear, I pull him backward into the bathroom. We don't even make it to a stall. I press him up against the sink, hands sliding under his T-shirt. His body is hot and it only takes a second before he's wrapping his legs around my hips and—

A toilet flushes. We freeze. Austin barely has a second to get his feet back on the ground before the second stall door opens and a tall blond man who I think is from the German snowboard team emerges. He gives us both a confused glance and I realize we're blocking the sink. We step out of the way and he washes his hands before wordlessly exiting the bathroom.

Fuck. I'm going to have to wait a few more minutes.

"Upstairs," I say.

"But we're supposed to—" Austin starts, but I don't care. Whatever other meeting he has with a doctor, therapist, or publicist can wait.

Except as the elevator doors open, we're met with Tara's potent scowl and ever-flawless eyeliner.

"Outside. Ten minutes. Don't forget." She steps between us as she exits the elevator.

This time my whine isn't so quiet. "But why?"

She might as well shoot laser beams from her eyes as she whirls. I duck behind Austin, ready to sacrifice my one true love in the face of her wrath.

"Apex is here. The whole team needs to be ready to go at three. It was on the schedule."

God fucking dammit. How do they manage to jam so many things into a single day?

The reps from Apex are here to do a final check on our race suits for competition. The process is tedious, because after the fittings comes the photos, and while it's not as elaborate as that photoshoot in Maine, somehow nearly three hours have still passed by the time I'm back in the elevator with Austin. My whole body feels infested with a thousand tiny ants, crawling over every inch of my insides. If I don't get to touch him, *really* touch him, in the next ten minutes, I'm going to turn to slush.

So of course, as I swing the door to my room open and shove Austin inside, Matthieu is coming out of the bathroom. Wasn't he at the fitting? His hair is wet like he's recently showered, and he's dressed like he's going somewhere, in clean pants and a black half-zip.

"What are you doing here? How did you get back so fast?" I was hoping if we hurried, we'd have a few minutes alone before my very much unwelcome roommate made it back. Isn't he supposed to be like a hundred years old by now? Shouldn't he have a bad knee that keeps him from moving too quickly? Any old sentiment about Matthieu's greatness as a competitor vanishes with the realization my veteran roommate is a massive cockblock and doesn't even know it.

Matthieu's eyes narrow and dart between the two of us. Then he says seven words that make my heart drop.

"You're coming to the team dinner, right?"

Fuuuuck. Why? Why would they schedule one of those for tonight?

"Austin's not—I can't—I have to—" I think I'm trying to tell him that Austin has some cryptic pain. A lingering something or other from his injuries that precludes dinner but will mysteriously be better by morning. And of course, I have to stay behind because clearly I am the only one who can take care of him.

Austin squeezes my hand and the silent consolation makes me want to cry.

"I'm going to take a quick shower," he says.

So we go to the ridiculous team dinner. It's at a local restaurant up the hill from our hotel. The whole team—ski, snowboard, support staff—gathers around long tables pushed together. There are no menus, and someone's clearly talked to the kitchen, because while the food is all rustic Italian, it's obviously been put together in consultation with our nutrition team. Steamed vegetables, trout with herbs and lemon, or veal that isn't drowning under inches of cheese and heavy tomato sauce. People take photos, post them on Instagram.

I taste none of it.

Somehow, Austin and I get seated across from each other, when clearly he should be beside me. He spends the night chatting with a couple of skiers from the women's team. I sit between Matthieu and Kage.

"Cedric?" Kage says at one point, though the way he taps my shoulder indicates maybe he's said my name a few times and I didn't hear him.

"What?" I ask, not meaning to be quite so stern, but Austin's laughing at something Marissa, who's sitting next to him, said, and even this moment of inattention makes me want him more. We've been apart for months, and every second the separation continues now is agony.

"Can you pass the bread?" Kage asks, though he might as well be speaking Lithuanian, because none of the words register.

Matthieu huffs on my other side, passing the basket of thickly sliced multigrain bread across my field of vision towards Kage. I duck, trying not to lose my line of sight with Austin.

"Should I find somewhere else to sleep tonight?" Matthieu asks. His mouth is so close to my ear that the words make me gasp and jump, finally breaking my concentration. I turn toward him, the protest already forming on my lips because I'm expecting him to be teasing. For there to be a turn to his lips. But his expression is all seriousness. He's not joking. He's offering.

I have to take a sip of the dark red wine we've been served before I speak.

"Would that be okay?"

He shrugs. "Kage talks in his sleep, but I've got earplugs. Better than listening to you two go at it like hyenas like I had to last year in Maine."

My ears feel like they burst into flames.

"Wh-what?" I stammer.

"The walls at that resort were very thin, Cedric. Did you think there was no one next door?"

Somehow, even though I've hardly thought of anything else but that night and the awful day after in the months that followed, questions like, "Did anyone overhear our marathon fuckfest?" have never crossed my mind. Maybe they would have if the next day had been a normal one. The kind with jokes and laughter as Austin and I raced each other down the hill, then raced even faster back to the hotel to pick up where we had left off. But all we had at the end of that day was broken bones and broken hopes.

I press my lips together, bunching my napkin in my lap. I'm not usually one for embarrassment, but knowing Matthieu heard us that night . . . I wasn't worried about being overheard. Sometimes I was trying to be as loud as possible. I wanted the world to know Austin was mine and I was his.

"We'll be quiet," I say. Matthieu pats my shoulder in a fatherly way, but it takes several minutes and the rest of my glass of wine before I can look at him again.

As dinner wraps up, Ivan rises and makes a short speech. He's not one for big demonstrations.

"You all know what we're here to do," he says. "You've worked hard to be here. I believe every one of you has it in you to win here. Stick with the program, and we'll see what happens." He lifts a glass and we all do as well. "Clear heads and strong legs. Be ready for your final runs tomorrow, remember to rest and hydrate tonight, and stay sharp."

I glance at Austin, and for the first time tonight, he's watching me too. His eyebrow arches and he tugs at his bottom lip with his teeth. The message is very clear. The odds of me being properly hydrated by the time the sun rises tomorrow morning are very, *very* slim.

CHAPTER
EIGHTEEN

WE TRY TO BE QUIET. Honestly, we do. The Olympics are notoriously horny, or so I've heard, but everyone else on the team must have taken a vow of celibacy until after the racing is done, because most people keep to themselves as we all walk down the wintery road from the restaurant back to the hotel, and voices are muffled while we head for the elevators. Austin and I get in first, then are nearly crushed as the whole team tries to squeeze in together. Small European elevators are not made for a whole Olympic entourage, but even once a few people step off, the two of us are squished into a back corner facing each other. My shoulder is jammed awkwardly to one side, trying not to push against one of the equipment techs. Austin's got a foot planted between mine and a hand on my waist. We do our best to look anywhere but at each other, but in my struggle to avoid Austin's gaze, I land on Matthieu and Kage's together, standing close towards the front. Kage smirks. Matthieu winks. I shift, trying to escape their silent teasing, but all that gets me is pressed even closer to Austin. So close, in fact, I can feel the thick ridge of a needy erection pushing against the front of his pants and grinding against my hip.

As people get off on each floor and the crowd in the elevator thins out, I push him gently behind me. The pants I wore to dinner are less fitted than his, and while I'm almost definitely just as hard, I can hide it better.

"Remember that end-of-season pizza party when we were twelve?" I whisper over my shoulder.

"What?" he asks. At least he's not grinding against my ass, but his hands are on each of my hips and his breath washing over the back of my neck makes me shudder.

"Lyle De Brun. Overdid it on chocolate cake and orange soda."

Austin groans and I know exactly the scene he's picturing. Poor Lyle. He was a few years behind us and way more interested in the after-practice snacks than he ever really was in racing. When presented with unlimited two-litre bottles of soda and a giant chocolate sheet cake, he couldn't control himself. After a few hours of stuffing himself silly without parental supervision, he suddenly exploded into a convulsion of orange and chocolate vomit that went on far longer than a typical child should be able. Fortunately we were outside, so he threw up into the snow. Unfortunately, Austin and I happened to get a front row seat, since we'd been assigned to clean-up crew, and were dumping empty paper plates into the garbage bin that had been Lyle's target before his stomach decided it had waited long enough and unleashed its wrath five steps away. The scene was out of a horror movie. The smell . . .

Oh hey. Erection's gone. And based on the way Austin drops his forehead to my shoulder and sags his whole body against mine so there's no space between us, his has evaporated too.

"You're the worst," he mutters.

I take the hand that's on one of my hips and wrap it around my middle, patting gently.

"You love me," I say, and I'm so confident in the words I don't even need his confirmation.

When the door dings for our floor, Matthieu takes off down the hall at a run.

"Where's he going?" Kage asks, as the rest of us exit. We walk down the hall at a more leisurely pace, and before Austin and I even get back to my room, Matthieu is letting himself out through the door again, a black toiletry kit tucked under one arm.

"Needed my toothbrush," he says, jostling the kit slightly. "Sleep tight."

"Sleep tight?" Kage asks, expression confused. "Where? Where are you sleeping?" His questions continue as Matthieu drags him back down the hall. He keeps glancing at us, but Matthieu continues until they reach the room Kage has been sharing with Austin and disappear inside.

"He's sweet," I say. "Not the sharpest edge on the ski, but a good kid."

"He's fast," Austin says. "Another couple years and we'll have a hard time keeping up with him."

No more race talk. I have spent all day being an Olympian and doing Olympic things. Now is the time to do something for us.

"I'll be slow," I say as I pull him into the room and let the door swing shut again. I'm trying to control myself, but my hands and my breath both shake.

"Slow?" he asks, tugging at the bottom of my shirt.

"I just . . ." I force more air in and out of my lungs, but I can't help myself when I reach for him to pop open the top button of his pants. "I really want you, Austin. Like, *really*. Like if I don't get to fuck you in the next five minutes, I may die of frustration. But you don't remember and—"

He kisses me. It's a mess of lips and tongues and teeth. He threads his fingers into my hair and pulls hard enough I whimper.

"What did I tell you about treating me like I'm breakable?" He growls the words into my mouth.

I'm already turning him and walking us toward the bed.

"Don't," I say.

"Right," he says, still kissing, but he breaks away long enough to pull his shirt over his head, then finishes my work by undoing the rest of his fly and shucking both pants and underwear, until he's standing in a puddle of clothes with his hands on his hips.

Holy shit.

If Austin from that night was fit—toned and strong from a whole season of competition—then the version of him that has spent the last ten months doing daily rehabilitation and training, working side by side with some of the best doctors and trainers in the country, is absolutely shredded. Muscles I've never seen before on myself or any of my teammates ripple under his skin. Tendons and veins strain as he lets me inspect every inch of him. His dick stands straight out from his body, bobbing gently. Also, as I sink to my knees in front of him, I find the raised scar on the outside of his ankle. And the similar one on the inside of his wrist.

"From surgery?" I ask, running my thumb over each.

He swallows hard. I probably shouldn't ask. He doesn't want me treating him differently because of the accident, and making him list his scars will only kill the mood.

But his hand goes to his ribs and he puts the pad of one finger to his side, then takes my hand and guides me to the same place. The scar there is smaller, hardly bigger than my fingertip, but the firm circle is noticeably different than the skin around it.

"From the chest tube. It was nearly a week before I could breathe on my own, or that's what they told me anyway. I don't remember."

I kiss it. Each of them. Side, wrist, ankle. The knobby lump where his collarbone knitted itself back together. I say a silent *thank you* to whatever god or spirit looked over us that day and in the weeks after and decided Austin got to live.

Slowly, he sits down on the edge of the bed, taking me with him. We kiss like that for a while, him sitting down, me on my knees. I let my hands wander. Scars again, the fine hairs on his arms, the flat shape of his nipples. He cups my face, looking into my eyes like I'm something precious.

"I really missed you," I say. Then, before I say anything else too vulnerable, I drop my head and take his cock in my mouth.

"Oh. Zed." He gasps as I let my tongue run over the underside of his shaft, finding the long vein that runs there.

"Bear," I say, letting him go long enough to speak.

"What?"

I'd forgotten until this very second about the different pet name. Not a nickname. Something for the two of us.

"You called me Bear. Back then."

He draws a thumb over my lips before guiding me back down to his dick. When I take him this time, his gasp is followed by a long low sound, before he says, "Bear."

It's all I need. Even if he doesn't remember, it's the tie back to that night. That other hotel room. That other life when I was sure we were on a direct path to our dreams. No interruptions. No distractions. I was so wrong in ways that old version of me could never have guessed. But it doesn't matter. Not anymore. We're back on track.

I work fast. I've been waiting all day. All year. My whole life, maybe—though probably not. The nine-year-old version of me who met Austin that day at junior ski team didn't know sucking on another man's penis was something people did for fun. Or that someday I'd be doing it with the kid I was about to swear eternal hatred for when he beat me on the hill. Except he's not a kid now, and holy shit his fingers back in my hair and the soft sound of his careful breathing is the biggest turn-on I have ever experienced.

"Bear. Jesus, Bear, don't stop."

I work him harder, taking him deeper in my throat, forcing myself not to gag. My nose is buried in his groin and he smells like soap and the faint scent of sweat. And himself. Austin. I've known him forever. Known him like this once before, but it's even better.

I slide back up so I can take in a fresh breath. I swipe my tongue over his slit and he moans. I could lick him like the sweetest treat all night long.

"I'm gonna come," he says, gripping the base of his shaft. "I wanna come in your mouth. Can we do that?"

We can do whatever he wants. I stay where I am, focusing on the drops that bead on his slit and the sensitive skin over his flared tip. He lies backward, arms spread out like a sacrifice. His abdomen rises and falls and for a second I hesitate, thinking about the lung that kept trying to fail him and how lucky he is that he gets to breathe at all.

"Don't stop," he says, voice shaky, bringing me back to the task at hand.

I don't stop. Not when his breathing turns into short, sharp gasps. Not when his hips start rocking in time with the slide of my lips over his shaft. Not when he lets out a strangled sound, fist against his mouth, as his dick pulses and jerks and shoots against the back of my throat. I swallow and gag. Tears squeeze reflexively from the corners of my eyes. He's hot and salty and I swallow every drop, keeping it safe. I'll keep all of him safe.

Austin shakes and twitches as I crawl up his body, kissing here and there. Older scars from our teenage mishaps. Freckles. The laser cat tattoo. I pull one of his nipples between my teeth and his whole body ripples with pleasure.

"Did you learn about that last time?" he asks.

Doesn't matter what I did and didn't learn. We can learn it all again together.

There's more kissing. Fumbling. It's slower than last time, almost like we knew we only had that night. It felt like we had to say everything and show each other everything we could do. Now it feels like I can pace myself. Like if there are places I don't get to explore or positions we don't get to try, there will be other opportunities. You never know when life will send you hurtling into a dense forest and smash you against a rock, but I have to believe that we've gotten through that part, and now we have time.

When we're finally ready, with me kneeling between his thighs and Austin with his legs pulled up against his chest and his slick hole ready for my entrance, I pause, holding the base of my cock tight, telling it to wait just one more second.

"I love you," I say. "I've been in love with you forever. I just didn't know it then."

His smile is a million expressions at once. Pleased. Smug. Shy.

"You don't have to say it back," I continue quickly. "I know you don't remember and I haven't . . . been a great friend lately. If you want tonight to be about pre-race nerves and letting some stress out, then—"

"Zed. Bear. I love you. I did then, and I still do now." His voice is fierce. Sure, I could flop forward and kiss him until we're both dizzy, but I need something else right now. Without more breathless words, I hitch his leg over one shoulder and slide into him. Our simultaneous sighs are deep and satisfied. We've needed this. Waited months and months for it. I kiss the base of his calf. Feel the thin hairs over his thigh.

"Okay?" I ask as I slide back out.

He nods.

"Okay. Then three . . ."

Austin's confident expression clouds. "What?"

"Two."

He laughs, covering his face. "You can't be serious."

I don't give him a one. We don't need it.

CHAPTER
NINETEEN

WE DO SLEEP. Eventually. Ivan would be pissed if we showed up for the last day of pre-race prep completely exhausted. I wake up tangled in Austin. Arms, legs, hair, breath. It's hard to tell where he starts and I end. His head rests on my chest.

"Morning," he says as I run my fingers over his scalp. His voice is heavy and sleepy. Rich, like good coffee. I want to hear it like that every morning for the rest of my life.

"I miss your long hair," I say. "It was very rugged."

He lets his own hand trail over my naked chest. "I liked it too, but I broke my wrist and collarbone. Basic things like brushing my hair were hard for a while. I can grow it out again now."

A sizzle of regret shoots through my chest. I should have been there. I could have brushed his hair. Ivan even gave me the chance to go, but I was too hurt—in my own way—to accept what he was offering.

But before I can start to second guess, a knock comes on the door, making us both jump.

"Cedric?" Matthieu's familiar accent comes through the wood. "Let me in."

I groan, but we've had our time. If I'd been here from the beginning with the rest of the team and Austin and I had figured our shit out sooner, we might have found time to get our rooms changed over so we could share this one and Matthieu could bunk properly with Kage. But today is not the day for shuffling suitcases and belongings back and forth.

It's the day before the Olympics, and we're on Ivan's time now.

We take one more trip up the mountain to do a final few passes over the course and inspect the conditions. It's warmer today than yesterday, though still well below freezing. A fine dusting of snow has come down overnight, enough to make the surface grittier than the day before, but there's no further precipitation in the forecast, so once all the competitors and coaches have spent their allotted time going over last-minute things, what's fallen will be packed down onto the base. Tomorrow should be free and clear.

At one point, I'm standing in the finish area, listening for Austin to come over the final ridge. My eyes are closed, my hands out in front of me as I visualize every turn and jump, playing over and over the line I need for maximum speed in the corners and where the best opportunities to pass a leader will be.

The scrape of sharp edges on hard snow has me opening my eyes as Austin rockets down the last pitch. We may not be allowed to go hard today, but Austin's only ever had one speed—bat-out-of-hell. If I'm going to win tomorrow, I need to ski perfectly to gain the advantage over him.

As he finishes his run, my attention drifts back up the final downhill, picturing us together. Just like we always said. Neck and neck, right to the line. Who wins? No one knows. They look at pictures and check timers and even after everything, it's so close that—

"Oof." Strong arms wrap around me as Austin comes up behind me, skis sliding to a stop outside mine. He kisses my cheek. "How was my time?"

"Stop," I say, squirming free.

He laughs. There's no hurt there. It's not that I care if people find out we're together. Just not today. There can be no distractions for the next twenty-four hours.

After the last runs, we spend time in the equipment tent, doing final inspections of everything. Skis, bindings, boot bails, pole grips. There are backups for everything, but you never want it to get to that. By the time you realize the tension on your bindings is off, the race will be over and you'll be at the back of the pack.

We don't ski anymore, but there are rounds of mobility and strength work to do. Competition day is brutal. Skiers who make it all the way to the Big Final will have competed in four races where placement can be decided by fractions of a second. The afternoon is for fine tuning. Activating the muscles that need to be ready for tomorrow. Stretching the muscles we'll push to their limits. At one point, Austin's doing gentle lunges with a resistance band. He's got his hands on his hips, but suddenly they shoot out to the air as he struggles to keep his balance.

"You okay?" one of the trainers asks.

"Yeah. No problem." Austin waves him off and the trainer moves on to watch someone else. When he's gone, Austin reaches behind himself to cup his ass, then glances over his shoulder to glare at me as he mouths, "Your fault." I blow him a kiss and he flips me off before he resumes his reps.

Another round of physio and massage. Felix takes one look at the two of us as we walk into the therapy room, shakes his head, and points through an open door.

"Cold tub," he says.

"No," I groan. I hate the cold tub. Sure, it helps with inflammation and such, but that shit fucking hurts.

"I'm not dealing with both of you in the same room again."

Kage, who is coming in behind us, snorts.

"Try sleeping down the hall from them," he says, then trips over his own feet when Austin gives him a playful shove.

So next thing I know, I'm in the ice bath, gritting my teeth both to ward off the stabbing pain as my whole body contracts, and also the terrible and tempting sounds of Austin once again groaning in the next room as the therapists work out the kinks. When he walks in a few minutes later, his face is flushed and he's shaking out his arms and legs before doing a few test squats, then smiles in my direction.

"I feel so much better," he says.

"I hate you so much right now." I pull myself out of the tub, being sure to shake like a dog when I'm back on solid ground. Austin laughs as he tries to dodge the spray, then yells when the ice-cold droplets hit his skin anyway. I reach for a towel, snapping it in his direction and he crashes into the tub in his effort to get away, making water slosh against the side.

"Knock it off, you two!" Felix shouts from the other room. We laugh louder to piss him off, but I exit quickly and let Austin have his soak.

Dinner is a quieter affair than last night. Team dinners are never held the night before competition—not the official ones, anyway. There are no fried veal cutlets tonight. No wine. Everything has been considered and prepared to give us the nutrition we need for tomorrow. The mood around our table is tense. I'm pretty sure Kage excuses himself to go throw up at one point. When he gets back, he's the colour of old milk, takes one look at his plate, then pushes it away.

"You have to eat," Matthieu says, sliding the meal right back at him.

Kage shakes his head, burping quietly. "I can't. I can't stop thinking about—" We all jump when the table shakes, but Kage jumps the highest. Then he scowls at Matthieu and practically whines. "What did you kick me for?"

"Because now you're not thinking about tomorrow. Eat your dinner."

Kage sulks for a few more seconds, but slowly he picks up his fork and pokes at his food. It's chicken tonight. Not much seasoning. Salt causes dehydration. The vegetables are steamed. The pasta is whole grain, which would probably make the Italians around us go into shock, but the dieticians and cooks are doing what's best for the team, not for the host country.

The air in the hotel is tense after dinner. Conversations are hushed. More than one athlete from Canada as well as from other countries can be found doing the strange silent dance I did while I waited for Austin at the bottom of the run. They stand or sit with their eyes closed, arms in front of them as they picture every inch of the course and the path that will take them to victory.

Too bad that gold medal is mine.

Curfew comes at nine, lights out at ten. Yes, we're all adults, but there's no wiggle room on this one. Matthieu graciously sleeps in Kage's room again. Austin and I lie together, awake but quiet.

This is it. The big game. The goal posts. This time tomorrow, one of us will be an Olympic champion.

"I'm totally going to kick your ass tomorrow," I say.

Austin snorts. "As if. You could never beat me when the chips were down."

"What?" I squawk and push up on an elbow. "Since when? Where were you when I was the top-ranked Canadian for three straight races two years ago? You know what top Canadian means, right? Oh yeah. I was the fastest. You've never been higher than number two on the leaderboard, regardless of who's on top."

"Shh," Austin laughs and pulls me down, quieting my protest with a kiss. "And who took your top seed and sent you to third?"

I laugh against his mouth. "Not you." Not only him, anyway. My ranking lasted for over a month before Matthieu came storming through in France and reclaimed his crown. Austin caught me eventually, pushing me back to third place on the team. It's always been like that. Back and forth, up and down, but never far apart. He's got the talent. I've got the strategy. Tomorrow really could be anyone's race.

"Bear," Austin says softly, rolling into me so I can slide an arm under his head and hold him close for a minute. There's no sex tonight. We don't even have to talk about it. There are old wives' tales about how orgasms are bad luck the night before a race or a competition. About how it steals your masculine energy or some other bullshit. Our restraint has nothing to do with that. It's that we both know that when we get started, we won't stop. Not for hours. Not until we're exhausted and sweating and everything has been used up. And that is not how we want to go into the morning of the biggest race of our lives.

"Yeah?" I answer.

He snuggles in closer. I press my nose against the top of his head, breathing him in. I can't fuck him, but I can hold him, and that's pretty amazing too.

"I hope you win tomorrow," he says.

I lift my head. "What?"

"It's like we always said. You and me. Together to the finish line. But I'm lucky to even be here. I want to win, but if it comes to it, and you see your chance, don't hold back for my sake. I'm not here to finish some story about my epic comeback."

"But you're here to compete," I insist. He has to be. The plan doesn't work if he's only here to enjoy the experience.

"Of course," he says, voice serious. "I'm going to do everything I can to win. But I need to know you're going to too. Don't treat me like I deserve it more or that somehow the accident means I've earned it. If I'm going to win, I want it to be because I left you in my rearview."

I lie back down, waiting for my racing heart to calm. We're saying the same thing. Neck and neck. Ski to ski. That's how he wants it to be. No more guilt. No more second guessing.

We fall asleep. I don't know what time it is. I wake up in the middle of the night and we're spooned together with my arm wrapped around him protectively.

Don't treat me like I deserve it more.

He doesn't. He's incredible, and he's worked so hard to get here. Harder than anyone. But I've worked hard too. I survived a shit season and nearly losing my best friend, and somehow I'm sleeping wrapped around him and waiting for the race that has defined my life to date.

I'm not going to treat him like he's fragile or that somehow he's more worthy because of everything that's happened.

I'm going to leave him in my wake, and slide over that finish line as number one in the world. There was only ever going to be one winner between us, and it's going to be me.

TWENTY

THE MORNING of my first Olympic Games, I wake up lying back-to-back with my best friend. My boyfriend. Our spines rest against each other, and I leave my eyes closed as I focus until our breathing is synced up. I imagine a loop, air moving from his lungs to mine and back again, sustaining us, connecting us.

"Are you awake?" Austin's voice is quiet, but it doesn't have that sleepy quality from yesterday. He's been up for a bit.

"Yeah," I say, rolling over so I can kiss his shoulder. Or that's the plan, but when I roll, so does he, onto his back, with his phone held over his face.

"We have a problem," he says, then flips the phone in my direction. My eyes are still bleary from sleep and I have to rub them a few times to get them to focus, but when I do, I see me and Austin, standing side by side, looking kinda derpy in our matching team jackets.

"Oh hey," I say, taking the phone and sitting up. "Did the interview go live?"

"No. I mean yes. But it's . . . it's not . . ." He doesn't need to explain. I scroll farther down and there's another picture from the interview. We're lying in the snow, face to face. Holy shit, that's hot. Like even someone who didn't know our story might look at it and go "those two boys aren't totally straight and possibly also want to do dirty things to each other behind closed doors." Or else you'd think we're just really good friends, but you'd have to be willfully ignorant to stick to that story.

I snort. "Funny they included that part. I thought they'd cut it after . . ." The thought dies on my tongue. There's another block of text, but below that is a picture not from the interview. It's the two of us, in our regular training wear, face to face and mouth to mouth. No matter how an observer might have interpreted the previous picture, there's no chance anyone could deny that in this one we're kissing.

The bottom corner of the picture is cut off at a weird angle, until I realize I'm looking at the white edge of that flap I thought was so conveniently protecting us from prying eyes outside the gear tent yesterday.

"Oh shit." I sit up quickly, zooming in the picture. The resolution isn't great. Definitely taken by someone with a cellphone and not a professional. But there's no question about what we're doing. No one would believe we were having a really intense conversation.

"Yeah," Austin says.

I scroll back up to the top of the article, to the title I didn't see above the first utterly harmless picture.

Canada's Ski-Crossed Lovers: Who Will Win?

I bet someone in the news room is real proud of coming up with that one.

My heart hammers in my throat as I read through the article. It's all there. Well, the publicly available details anyway. Austin's accident. My terrible season and last-minute fluke qualification. Then it talks about how we were spotted making out during practice, and how media members noticed palpable chemistry during an interview.

"Fucking Ray and Chantale," I growl, throwing the blanket off as I get out of bed and rummage through my stuff for clothes.

"Where are you going?" Austin asks, rising too.

"I'm going to find those two shithead influencer wannabes and tell them exactly what they can do with their 'content.' Are you coming or not?"

"Zed. Wait."

I'm not waiting. Why the fuck would I wait? This is our private lives. They don't get to splash it around for other people to gawk at.

I hop up and down, trying to get my shoes on. Austin's standing by the bed, wearing only his underwear and one of my T-shirts.

"Let's go," I say, stomping into my shoes. I mash the heel cup down, but I don't care.

"Cedric," Austin says, not following. "Bear. Stop."

I do. I'm shaking with rage, but at his use of the private name, my hand stops on the doorknob. I look over my shoulder at him. He's still rumpled. Austin rubs the scar from the surgery to repair his shattered wrist.

Finally, he says, "It's the Olympics. Our Olympics."

The air rushes out of me. I sag. "Fuck."

He comes up behind me, wrapping his arms around my body, holding me close until my breathing slows. He kisses the back of my neck.

"Let me get some fresh clothes. We'll go find Ivan. Maybe Tara. We'll figure this out. But we've also got to get ready for race time."

This was not how any of it was supposed to go. But I step back, letting Austin pull the door open. Then we both jump, because Matthieu is there, hand raised like he was about to knock.

"Oh," he says, sounding surprised. "You're awake. Did you . . . did you see the . . ."

"Yeah," I say, as Austin pushes past him, heading down the hall to his room. I take more steps back and slump onto the edge of my mattress.

Matthieu enters the room and lets the door close behind him.

"I'm sorry," he says, standing a few feet away. "People don't think. They forget we're really people. They were only thinking about themselves. About the views those pictures would get."

I shake my head. Now that my anger is subsiding, something like cold fear settles in my guts.

"I don't have time for this today. We had a plan. We've always had a plan, and this—" I gesture at my phone, which is still lying on its charger by my bedside. "How am I supposed to win today when that's . . . out there?"

Matthieu snorts. "You're not going to win."

My head snaps up. "What?"

His smile is crooked and his eyes are bright. "I'm going to win. That part was never in question."

I laugh in spite of myself, then flop down on the bed, rubbing my eyes.

"Fuck. It's been a mess since last year, but that . . . That was private."

"You and Austin have never been subtle." Matthieu sits on his bed, the one he hasn't slept in for the last two nights, and probably won't sleep in again before we finally leave Italy. He's a good teammate.

My sigh is heavy as I pull myself back up to sitting. "What do we do? What do *I* do? I don't want to deal with that. Not today."

"Then don't." He shrugs.

"But it's . . . it's everywhere." I pick up my phone, but even the sight of the notifications on the lock screen is enough to turn my insides to acid, so I put it down again. Social media tags. Text messages. How am I supposed to ignore that?

Matthieu holds out his hand. "Give me that." I do. He tucks it into the drawer of his bedside table. "I'll give it back after the race."

I want to protest. Tell him I don't need him to protect me. That I can handle it. But the way my hands are still shaking says maybe a little help wouldn't be so bad.

He must see the decision on my face, because he nods. "Good. Now put the rest of it away. Let people say and think what they want. You know what to do. You've trained for this. You know how to make these thoughts a problem for another time. Today is for racing and only for racing."

The longer he speaks, the heavier his accent gets, and I expect him to launch into a passionate speech fully in French any second now. That is, until a fresh knock comes at the door, interrupting him. It's Austin, with Tara and Ivan standing behind him, glowering like twin thunderstorms.

"I found them in the hall," he says, entering without further explanation.

"I'll let you talk," Matthieu says, leaving again.

There are a few seconds of awkward silence as the rest of us get settled. Ivan takes the single chair by the hotel room's desk. Austin and I sit side by side on my bed. Tara paces in tight circles.

"You don't have to worry about any of this," she says.

"Kind of hard not to," Austin says.

"She's right." Ivan looks like he wants to punch something, and leans back in his chair while he folds his arms over his chest to control himself. "This is her job to deal with. Today your only job is to race."

He sounds like Matthieu. They're probably right. What do we know? This is Matthieu's third games, and Ivan's raced in and coached at least ten. If they say this isn't our fight, we should listen.

"I've got it under control," Tara says. She has her phone out, texting furiously. "I've sent calls out to the Olympic Committee press office. The Chef de Mission. I sent someone down to the CSBC media hub to ask them what the goddamn fucking hell made them think that this bullshit clickbait horsesh . . ." She presses her lips together, giving us a guilty glance. Then she straightens, pulling her shirt down at the waist and smoothing over the front. At first glance, she's pressed and polished as always this morning. Only on closer inspection, her ponytail is lopsided, and while she's got some makeup around her eyes, it looks like it was scribbled on in a hurry instead of the usual painstaking application she must undertake most mornings. "Sorry. I have it handled. I've already requested extra security to keep the media away from the athlete's village and during pre-race warm ups. If anyone approaches you, all you say is 'no comment.' Understand?"

We both nod. But a thought tugs at the back of my mind.

"Don't you want to know if it's true?" I put my hand on Austin's thigh and he wraps his fingers around mine. We look up at Tara, a united front. We won't hide. We were never hiding. But we also weren't very smart about the whole thing.

Ivan coughs, but when I glance back at him, he's trying and failing to hide a smile. Tara rolls her eyes, still jabbing at her phone.

"Of course it's true. Anyone who has ever seen the two of you together wouldn't doubt that for a second. You just have really terrible timing. But don't worry. I've got your back. Don't say anything to anyone and do your best. I'll see you after seeding." Then she holds her phone to her ear, and her voice echoes after her as she walks out to the hall and disappears. "Roland? It's Tara. Yeah, I know. That's what I'm calling about. Listen . . ."

"I told you I wanted to tell you after the games," Austin mutters, staring down at his hands.

"You blabbed your secret last year," I remind him.

Ivan stands, the action requiring a long, tired grunt as he rises. He's undoubtedly thinking he doesn't get paid enough to deal with our bullshit. Not today especially, but never on any day, really.

"Should I go get Adiola?" he asks. We both shake our heads. She's not going to tell me anything I don't already know. We've been over this before. Maybe not *this* this. But the bigger part of her job, when she's not talking me through my guilt and mixed-up feelings about Austin's accident, is helping us learn all about compartmentalization and how to stay focused on racing even when there are a million other things going on in our lives. To the best of my knowledge, no one's ever been revealed kissing in national media before, but I know guys who have raced the day after a bad fall or after they get the news a loved one has passed away. This is no different. Focus on the job at hand. Deal with everything else on another day.

Ivan gives us a stoic nod. He's taught us well. Done everything to prepare us and give us the resources to not only get through today, but kick ass in the process.

"I'll see you downstairs for breakfast," he says, then leaves us alone to get ready for our Olympic morning.

CHAPTER
TWENTY-ONE

BREAKFAST IS SURPRISINGLY LOW-KEY. We get a few looks as we walk into the dining room. More than our team is eating, but even if the international crowd has seen the news and the pictures, no one here is going to waste precious attention and energy on the two dumbasses from Canada who couldn't be bothered to find a private place to make out. Like us, they have one of the biggest race days of their careers ahead. No one has time for us.

Matthieu and Kage are sitting together, and Matthieu pulls the chair closest to him out, prompting us to sit. Kage is looking better than last night. Well rested. Less green. He gives us a nervous glance, but Matthieu quietly clears his throat, and whatever question Kage was about to ask dies before he can set it free.

After breakfast, we do a final round of dressing, then ensure we have all the gear we'll need for the day. Extra gloves. Extra goggles. Dry socks. We've gone through this process a thousand times on different days at different mountains all over the world, and the act of checking my bag one more time helps to settle me. This is an important day, but it's only another day. Another race on another hill.

There are a few people with cameras waiting as we exit the

hotel, me and Austin side by side. But Tara's been good on her word and whatever media has managed to make it out to the hotel is being kept behind barricades by tall men in black coats that read *Sicurezzi* on the back—which I assume is Italian for "security"—while we load into the van. We sit together, thighs pressed against each other, but we don't talk. Austin's eyes are closed, and his hands move slightly as he mentally replays the run over in his head. I try to do the same, but my mind is a blank. No snow. No slopes. For a second, panic threatens to grab hold of my chest, but then a warm hand slides into mine.

"Stick to the plan," Austin says gently.

Right. The plan. When I close my eyes again, it's all there. Start. Jumps. Rises, falls.

We check in at the gate, showing them our credentials and waiting while our bags are inspected. Some of the other countries' athletes have already arrived. Others are in line behind us. Everyone is quiet. Focused on their day. Their race. No one cares about us except that we're two more people they'll have to ski faster than if they want to reach the podium.

After check in, we grab practice skis and take one more ride up the mountain as a team. Ivan's there. Matthieu and Kage. I was right. The conditions today are perfect. Cold and fast. No new snow. Just a packed, slick surface that will send us flying at top speeds all the way down the course. We go through it all one last time. The changes, the gates. Ivan points out the places where the shadows will be deepest for our seeding run, where the contrast will be poorest and we'll be most likely to make a mistake by misjudging the terrain. We should know it all by heart now, but with only split seconds to react to any slips once we're racing, a last round of preparation can't hurt anyone.

We come to the edge of the trail on the high side of a turn. Ivan's reviewing passing strategies. I'm staring down the far side of the mountain, where groomed trail gives way to dense trees and unseen hazards. I think about Austin losing control and flying over the side, disappearing into disaster.

"Hey." Like he knows what I'm thinking, he taps the back of my boot with his pole basket, making me turn away from imagined catastrophe. I blink until our gazes finally meet, and he shakes his head slowly. "Not today."

Not today. Risk is part of this sport. It's dangerous at any age and skill level. But we have done absolutely everything we can to be ready for today. Not only to be ready. To win. I'm going to leave him in my tracks and cross the line first. Every single race. Seeding to Big Final. That's the plan.

The morning stretches on for what feels like forever and rushes by in a blur. Video review. Strength and muscle activation. Another round of equipment inspection. Small meals meant to keep our energy up but never weigh us down. Sometimes I hear the click of a camera shutter or catch people watching me, then whispering to a companion. But when I turn, the camera is nowhere to be seen. And as for the whispers . . . they could be commenting how badass I look in my race suit.

Apex was there for that day everything changed, and for today, when it all comes together. When this is over, I'm going to talk to Tara about pitching me as a brand ambassador. Boy, do I have stories I can tell about my Apex experience.

Before real racing starts, we do the seeding run. Each person goes down solo. Your time determines which heat you'll be in for the round of thirty-two.

My run isn't bad. Hard and slick. I make a few mistakes, but nothing a viewer at home would notice on TV, and it's enough that I finish the run in fifth place with another twenty or so skiers to go behind me, including the rest of my team. Austin's only three people back, so I stick around to watch him do his run. The big screen at the bottom shows him coming through the jumps and turns and his form is perfect. He stays low and tight, and his extensions to keep his balance in the gnarly bits are controlled.

I'm in eighth place by the time he's done. He's in second, but with several hundredths of a second between him and the third-place finisher. Lots of room for other skiers to push us even farther apart before we start the heats.

"Did you go okay?" he asks as we push off on our skis, heading back to the lift.

I make a dissatisfied noise. "I've got some adjustments to make. But it'll be better next time. Turn two set me back, but I know what to look for."

We're all business. There's no time right now for sweet words or goofing around. This is what he meant when Austin said he was going wait to tell me he loved me. Right now we have no room for distractions.

Someone leaps in front of us, a woman with dark hair and a winter coat that includes a fur-lined hood. Not an athlete or anyone associated with the race. Spectator, then.

"Can I get a selfie?" she asks. "I read all about you this morning. You're so cute. Is it hard to be gay in ski cross? Are you the first two to come out?" She spins, holding her phone up to frame herself, along with our two shocked faces. Before she can take the picture, though, a man in an official games jacket steps forward, shouting in rapid staccato Italian. The woman may not understand the words, but the tone is clear. Get the fuck away from the athletes.

"No comment," Austin murmurs softly to himself, making me laugh. Where's Tara when you need her? She would have fully bodychecked that woman and tackled her into the snow.

When seeding is done, there's a short break while officials inspect the course, replace gates that were clipped by skiers, double check snow fences and such. We take the time to eat, hydrate, review footage one more time. The mood among our team is mixed. Austin finished seeding the highest, placing seventh. Matthieu is twelfth and I'm seventeenth. Kage is twenty-sixth and looks bummed about it. Matthieu sits next to him in the snow for a moment, speaking softly with him. There's only so much to say. The ranking doesn't mean a lot beyond which heat he'll start in. As long as he knows where he lost time and what he needs to do to not make the same mistakes again, he's got the same chance as anyone else.

I go in the first heat, which is not my favourite place to be. It gets the initial waiting over with, but then means there's a lot of waiting on the back end while the other seven heats run.

"You got this," Kage says, giving me a thumbs-up and a shaky smile. Austin gives me a quick nod and a fist bump. Matthieu is fiddling with his boots and doesn't say anything. Skiing is a solitary sport at the end of the day, even with three other men behind you.

I'm in the outside gate, which makes it harder to draft once the race gets going, but makes the starts easier, since I only have to fight one other competitor for position, though I still wind up third after we finish the rollers. The sun is up higher now, closer to midday, and the snow has softened somewhat. I keep my eyes downhill, looking for the opportunity to pass the lead skier to open. It does in the second turn. My line is better this time. Still high, but with more traffic since my last run, the terrain is better. It doesn't slow me down and by the time I come around to the next jump, I'm clear, moving through empty air alone, though the hiss of skis behind me says someone is close. The third turn is tight. If whoever is behind me gets any closer, they're going to clip my skis. Contact is inevitable in this sport, but it's especially tricky when you're the one out front and can't see what's coming. If I slow down to give him the room he's entitled to take to pass me, I might let all three of them go by at the same time.

In the final pitch, I'm second, crossing the line a hair behind an American skier. I'd have rather been first, but my time is better than my seeding run, and second is all I need to move onto the next round.

Austin's in the heat behind me, and he struggles at the top, trying to find a clear path, but the problem is solved for him when an Italian skier lands badly on the first jump and takes out two of his three competitors, leaving Austin with clear sailing all the way to the finish. It's not the way anyone wants to win a heat, but it happens in ski cross, and Austin is all smiles as he pulls up his goggles to check the big board with race results.

"Nice one," I say, offering a fresh round of fist bumps. I've lingered in the finish area again to watch his race. The crowd of spectators has grown since the seeding runs. People from all over the world wave different flags and ring bells and cheer for their favourites.

"Cedric! Cedric!"

I turn, and my mom is there, waving a red and white maple leaf with my dad. I gasp. They're supposed to be at home in Ottawa. How did they get here? They're cheering deliriously and I wave. I want to go to them, but not right now. It might have been better if I didn't know they were here at all. Stay in the game.

Austin's waving too, and that's when I realize his parents are there as well. He also doesn't approach. My mom snaps a picture, then a few other people around her do too. Then more. The Canadian contingent seems to realize who we are. No doubt they've all read the article. I think I hear someone shout "Kiss!" but before I can look to see who it is, Austin slides in front of me, jerking his chin toward the exit from the finish area. It's a silent command. Not now. There are still three more races to go. No time for diversions.

Except now that we're into true competition, the exit area is actually a media gauntlet. Reporters from each of the competing countries' major news outlets are waiting to get clips and sound bites from competitors. Normally, we wouldn't really need to do more than stop to talk to whoever is here from the CSBC, but as we approach, our names go up in a clamour. Phones and cameras are raised. If they can't talk to us, they at least want a picture. The ski-crossed lovers. I shouldn't have waited for Austin. Being seen together today is a stressor neither one of us needs.

He's hesitating too, staring down the chute of shouted questions. Then Tara steps in front of us, looking like a warrior going into battle.

"Follow me and do not stop," she says.

"Not at all?" I ask. Technically, we're required to at least stop for the CSBC. National duty and all that.

She whirls, glaring daggers at me. She's bundled up and looking far more polished than she did before six o'clock this morning. Hair in place. Eyeliner etched on. The purse of her lips is a hundred percent "do not argue or fuck with me" so I nod once and we follow as she hurries us through the line of reporters, shouting "No comment!" and waving her arms to make space as people volley questions in our direction. The Olympics really are a team effort.

Only, the last question catches my attention.

"What?" I ask, skidding to a halt. I turn so fast that the skis perched on my shoulder nearly take out a volunteer who has gotten a little too close in an effort to guide us back toward the lift area.

"Who's going to win in the next heat? You or Austin?" I don't recognize the journalist speaking, and her heavy accent says English isn't her first language, but her question is clear enough.

And that's when the realization hits me. Between my anxious wait for Austin to finish, then the sudden appearance of our parents, I didn't have a chance to think it through until now. We both survived our heats, but that means we'll be in the starting gate together in the next one. Four men, including the two of us. Two skiers will advance to the semifinal. Two will not. From here, it's a fifty-fifty shot that we'll both move on.

I glance at Austin. His face is blank, but the twitch in his cheek says he's doing the same math.

I say, "We're going to stick to our game plan. Ski our best race and see what happens."

We walk on. I expect Tara to scold me for saying anything, but once we're clear, she gives me an approving look.

"I've taught you well," she says. "Now don't do anything to fuck it up."

Then she melts into the crowd, no doubt on her way to do some more media damage control. We're all working hard today.

Austin and I stand still for a moment, watching the organized chaos unfolding around us. The spectators vying for a better place to see the racing. Officials and coaches moving here and there, talking into radios in a multitude of languages. Skiers heading back to the lift for another run, or standing at the bottom, realizing their day and their Olympic dream is already over. It's everything I imagined it would be. And it's not over for us.

"Let's go," I say, nudging him. From here on out, we have to be perfect. To be the two at the top of the podium this afternoon, we have to finish one-two in the next three races. No room for mistakes. No accidents.

It's time to put the plan into action.

CHAPTER
TWENTY-TWO

TWO CANADIANS WALK INTO A BAR. Actually, there were more of them. A whole ski team's worth, looking for some karaoke to let off steam after finishing their season. Some were looking to celebrate. Others to lick their wounds. They talked about the day, and the coming weeks and months of training and preparation. At some point, two Canadians walked out of that bar, confident in their future. So confident that one gave up on his plan to keep his feelings to himself until a more appropriate time and impulsively kissed his best friend.

And then our trail veered over the edge and plummeted into unknown and dangerous territory.

But somehow, we are now exactly where we always planned to be. Side by side in the gates. A lifetime of preparation putting me and Austin next to each other and going head-to-head. Only two advance. It has to be the two of us.

Our two rivals are from Japan and Sweden. They're good. Everyone here is good. As the Japanese skier works with his tech to get his boots clear to step into the bindings, I close my eyes, visualizing the race. I've done it twice already today. Three more and I'm golden. Beside me, Austin's doing jump squats, letting out explosive breaths to keep his body and mind alert.

The last thing we want is a second of hesitation when the start comes.

When the barrier falls, we drop onto the course and push over the rollers. Our arms and breaths come out perfectly synchronized. Japan and Sweden are on the far side. I can see Sweden out of the corner of my eye, but then we drop over the first rise. Austin comes with me, tucking in. Racing strategically is illegal. You can't block an oncoming racer to give a teammate an advantage. Not officially, anyway. But you can block him to hold your own space in the race, and Austin knows the plan. First and second don't matter, as long as it's the two of us together.

Someone's coming on my left. Not Austin, who is still crouched in tight behind me, drafting until he finds his chance to break out. I push us higher up the turn, hoping to force the passer into the softer untracked surface. The unseen person curses and grunts, but the sound of his skis fall away. We take off over a jump, so the only sounds I can hear are the wind in my ears and Austin's breathing behind me. Our takeoff was perfect, so our landing should be . . .

Whap.

. . .

Whap.

Shit. The interval between our landings is farther apart than it should be, and Austin's is quickly followed by the sound of two more. We're barely more than a second apart, all four of us.

Another figure appears in the corner of my vision, but the red bib makes me breathe. Austin. He's coming up alongside me. But with his approach comes the scrape of new skis as someone tries to ride his path past me. We're coming up to a small uphill section. I can't afford to lose any speed by pushing the others higher here. It's something we talked about during training this week. Instead, I tuck in tighter, trusting Austin can hold them off. Stick with the plan. All the training and practice. No space for doubt. We can do this.

As we come down the last section before the final pitch, the crowd is already roaring. There's no time to look. I'm still in front and Austin's beside me, but I have no way to be sure where the Japanese or Swedish skiers are. They're close. The last jump and how we land it will determine who moves on and who calls it a day.

Whap.

We all come so close together I can barely distinguish mine from the other three. The spectators scream and shout, bells ringing and whistles calling to us, bringing us down the last few seconds. My gaze is locked on the finish line. Nothing to do now but hold on. It's all happened in a blink.

I come to a stop in a spray of flying snow. Austin's right in front of me, wheeling around so we finally rest face to face. His mouth is open, chest in his tight-fitting race suit pumping hard as he fights for air.

"Did we do it?" I ask, though the question comes out as more a strangled gasp than anything intelligible. Our gazes swing to the board, straining to make out the results.

There's nothing. On the screen, a photo of the four of us coming over the line. We might as well be doing an acrobatic dance routine. The precision is so impressive. The crowd stills, murmuring in anticipation, but even from the picture it's hard to say for sure. Me. Maybe Austin? The Swedish skier can barely be seen, but I can't tell if that's because he's crouched next to one of us and invisible to the camera, or so far behind he's out of the frame that has captured a specific thousandth of a second.

A cry goes up, so loud it makes me jump before I go back to the leaderboard.

1. GRIMM, A (CAN)

2. BERARD, C (CAN)

3. OHASHI, S (JPN)

4. BERG, J (SWE)

The difference in our times is less than four tenths of a second.

My arms fly up on their own, and the shout that erupts from

my lungs is pure triumph. I might as well have won the whole thing. Beside me, Austin slumps over his poles, jamming them into his armpits to keep himself from pitching over entirely. Ohashi and Berg offer congratulations. Their race is done. We shake hands, then, once they've moved on to the media pen, high-five and celebrate a few seconds longer before we follow.

No Tara this time. Everyone has questions now. I repeat the same words over and over.

"I'm trying to race the best race I can."

"Everyone skiing at this level has a shot at winning it all."

"I'm focused on the next race, no further than that."

My head spins. It's a whirlwind, and the time between races gets shorter and shorter as the field gets cut by half.

We head to the lift and my stomach growls. Everything feels like it's happening too fast.

"You okay?" Austin asks, standing by my side as we wait for the chair to pass so we can push into the loading area.

"Yeah." Only I'm not. My pulse is racing. My brain is a tornado of thoughts and scenarios. I play a mental highlight reel of Ivan pointing out things to remember. Places where the run will get slower in the afternoon as the snow softens infinitesimally in the cold winter sun. The best places to pass and what to do when someone else knows the same thing and tries to pass you. I shake my head. "No. I'm not. Can you take the next lift?"

Austin doesn't question. He leans into his poles and watches as I slide into the loading area and sit back onto the chair.

The silence as I pull out of the base and rise into the air fills me with the same relief as the best orgasm of my life. I close my eyes. Focus on breathing. In for four, hold it for four, out for six, hold for four.

The litany of chatter between my ears fades away.

Fuck. For all this is another day on the mountain and another race, this is the most intense thing I've ever done. I glance over my shoulder. Austin's sitting in the chair behind. I give him a thumbs-up, and he responds with the same. We don't speak. The joking from the past days, Austin grabbing his ass and telling me the pain is my fault. It's all gone now. We are fully locked in.

Two more races.

Matthieu's out. Came third in his quarter final. I'm so focused on my race I don't even think to ask, but when we reach the top of the hill, Kage is there, standing alone and he tells us.

"But you qualified?" I ask.

He bites his lower lip. "There were two Americans in my quarter final. They took each other out in the chicane."

A win is a win. It could have just as easily been him wiping out through those tight turns.

At least he's not in our semi. Wouldn't it be wild if he made it to the Big Final and we had a one-two-three Canadian podium?

I shut my eyes and shake my head again. One run at a time. I can't be worrying about Kage's race.

There's a pause before the semis. One of the Austrian skiers takes a bad fall, though that's all we hear. No one wants the distraction of imagining injuries and the sight of ski patrol loading someone we've raced alongside all season and even for years into a sled. I have enough of that in my memories of Austin's accident.

Finally, though, we get the call. Ivan's been talking through our progress so far, reviewing video of our runs. Even the smallest adjustments can be the deciding factor between making the Big or Small Final now.

"You've got this," he says as the officials round us up.

Austin and I get placed on opposite ends of the gate. Between us are an Italian and a German skier. I allow myself one look down the line as we get into position, but all I can see are Austin's knuckles wrapped around the handles as he waits for the start.

The barrier drops as I'm still turning my attention forward. Fuck. I push off fractions of a second behind the others, cursing and swearing inside my head the whole time. Fuck. It's not even one race now. One feature. Rollers. Jumps. Don't worry about the finish line when we're barely through the start.

But I'm still on the inside, and somehow as we drop out of the rollers, I'm ahead, even if only by half a ski length. I take a deep breath, re-centering myself. One turn. One heartbeat, then the next.

The German is right on my ass. He's beaten me before. Recently, though that's not saying much given the state of my World Cup season this year. I hit the first jump in the exact spot Ivan and I discussed and come down fast, building my lead. He's still there, though, hovering behind my shoulder, waiting for his moment.

Where's Austin?

We go through the chicane, where Kage's Americans fell. I push hard, risking a little contact to force the German off his line. He grunts, but stays close, slipping farther back. Someone else is coming up. For a second, I think I see the red and grey of Austin's race suit, but I can't be sure. The German comes up beside me as we do the uphill, then falls away when he takes the next jump later than he should. I'm back on the snow and moving fast before he lands.

In the distance, the bells ring, urging me on.

Austin. He's there, right? I can't hear or see him. Not for sure. It's lost in heartbeats and breath, the scrape of skis on hard packed snow and the grunts as we take flight again and come down hard.

The last pitch. I'm alone out front. Holy shit. This is the biggest lead I've had all day. Nothing to do now but bring it home.

A flicker of motion comes up in the corner of my eye. Then the German blows past me, crossing the line only millimetres ahead. He throws his arms up in victory and I watch in shock.

He came first. So I came second. And that means . . .

I whip myself around, looking back up the hill. It should be empty. Fractions of a second. That's what separates first and fourth place. By the time I look, Austin should be over the line.

Only there's only three of us down here in the finish area. I look back up the hill and spot the form on the snow, two thirds of the way down the final descent. He's missing a ski and finishing a spiralling fall that leaves him face down in the snow.

It's Austin.

TWENTY-THREE

I DON'T THINK. Nothing that happens next is in the plan. One second, I'm watching, gasping, at the sight of Austin's body finishing a spectacular tumble. The next, I'm already out of my skis and running back over the finish line.

He's down. He might be hurt. I didn't see him fall. Again.

But before I can even get ten steps up the hill, he's sitting up. Course officials run out from where they've been observing the races. He's already halfway to standing by the time they reach him. He waves, to them and then to us, letting us know he's all right.

I drop to my knees. My whole body shakes as I watch Austin push himself along on one ski until he comes to where the other finally came to a stop after it popped off. He steps into it, waving his arms over his head again as he makes the final slide down the hill. I watch as he slips past me, crossing over the finish line. The crowd cheers for him anyway, and I stumble after him. He pulls off his helmet and goggles, and he turns as I approach him. His smile and eyes are bright, cheeks flushed.

"You stupid fucking asshole," I say, not stopping my advance until my hands plant firmly onto his chest, shoving at him as I try to relieve the riot of emotions burning hot under my skin.

He says something like, "I know," before he folds me into his body and kisses me.

It's the sort of thing they immortalize in vintage photography and classic art. His strong arms wrapped around me, while mine are crushed awkwardly between us. His mouth is hot and hungry on my lips, and the cry that goes up from the spectators as they watch our display is thunderous. We stay like that for what feels like a lifetime. Kissing. Touching. Apologizing and promising everything without saying a word. When we finally break apart, my head is spinning for entirely new reasons.

"Are you okay? Like, really okay?" I ask. I'm still shaking, but feeling sturdier than I did a few minutes ago.

"Fine," he says, though he grimaces as he tilts his neck to one side. "Nothing Felix and his torture ice bath can't fix."

I push at him again, laughing. Over his shoulder, all our parents are watching. Our moms cling to each other, and I think my dad might be crying. Fuck. I'm not even done racing yet.

But Austin won't be there.

"No," I say, the sound utterly heartbroken. "No. The Big Final. You didn't—"

"It's okay." His smile is crooked. There's no pain in his eyes, either physical or emotional. "That I even made it here is a miracle. I've still got the Small Final. And I've got you." He turns me, so I'm facing the exit and the waiting journalists who must now be drooling for a chance to talk to us after our little display here. Austin gives me a gentle push toward them. "Go. Go win the whole thing."

I trip over the rigid toes of my boots but regain my balance before I fall and make a complete ass of myself. I find my abandoned skis and poles, then find Tara waiting for me, tapping a manicured nail on her arm as she waits for my next pass through the media run.

"Are you two finished?" she asks, though her eyes flicker with what I hope is amusement and not barely controlled violence.

I laugh. "Not even a little bit."

She rolls her eyes. "Well, the no-comment strategy is out the window, but I'd still suggest that you not—"

I don't wait to hear her advice. Instead, I slip into my skis to more quickly make my escape through the reporters. They all lean in as I approach, hurling questions at me, but I slide past them, not stopping to answer a single one.

"I'll see you at the finish line," I call. Let them do with that soundbite as they will. Regardless of what happens in this last race, my new catch phrase won't be what gets reported tomorrow. The kiss. Austin's arms wrapped around me. No one will remember how many times I told them about one race at a time.

A few minutes later, I'm in the equipment tent, waiting while the techs examine my skis. There's a bigger break now than there has been between the other qualification rounds. A chance to inspect gear and swap out for fresh layers. Rehydrate and eat. Maybe even a quick stretch with the trainers to work out muscles that have already been pushed to the limit in the seeding round and first three runs of the day. Anyone who has made it to this point in the day is already aching, and now the most important race of all looms.

"I did it!"

With zero warning, an unexpected body hurtles into me, wrapping his arms around my middle. He's smaller than Austin, and when he pulls his head back to look up at me, it's Kage.

"Holy shit. Breathe," I say. In fact, he's breathing so hard he's going to pass out if he doesn't get it under control. "What's going on?"

"I did it," he says, face shining with uncontained excitement. "I made the Big Final!"

I blink, trying to unpack his words. I was so caught up in Austin and I not getting there together, I forgot about him. Matthieu is out, and in my narrowing focus, I had completely forgotten about Kage.

Now, though, I whoop, high-fiving him.

"The Big Final!" I call. We do a few celebratory hops before I spot Ivan lurking in the tent's entry. When our eyes meet, he waves us over.

"How are you both feeling?" he asks, his voice all business.

"Amazing!" Kage says, still sounding on the verge of hyperventilating. I nod in agreement. In all honesty, I'm starving, and there's a knot behind my shoulder blade that needs to be worked out ASAP. But I don't want to dampen Kage's enthusiasm. He's worked as hard as any of us to get to this point. I'm still going to kick his ass in the last race, but that doesn't mean he can't celebrate reaching the Olympic Big Final in only his second year of senior competition.

Ivan brings us back to order. Food. Electrolytes. More video review. I'm lucky the German didn't pass me sooner in that last race. My focus was so obviously all over the map through the middle of the course as I tried to figure out where Austin was, and it could have cost me everything. Felix appears with a massage gun that must be used to elicit confessions out of even the most hardened criminals, but by the time he's done, the knot in my shoulder is gone.

I'm doing start simulations with a resistance band when a soft voice comes behind me.

"Hey."

It's Austin. He's still in his race suit. He may have fallen, but making it to the semis guaranteed him at least a spot in the Small Final.

I've been so locked in on what comes next, I forgot that even still had to happen.

It's my turn to kiss him. I reach out, hand behind his head to bring his mouth to mine. The nervous energy under my skin needs a release valve, and Austin's soft groan against my lips turns me to liquid. Who cares who sees? Apparently everyone important knew already anyway. They knew more than Austin, who had forgotten everything. What a year this has been.

I pull away before we get ahead of ourselves and let out a slow stream of air that whistles between my teeth.

"How long until you go to the start?" I ask. The Small Final will happen first. There are no consolation prizes. No participation medals. But coming fifth or sixth at the Olympics is so far ahead of the millions of people who put on a pair of skis every winter simply for the enjoyment of being outside in the fresh air and cold, it's still worth doing properly.

"Three minutes," he says, keeping his face close to mine.

Not enough time for anything fun. Who cares what the wives' tales say? We've made it this far, and our dream of standing on the podium together is over. A quick hand job behind a tree or in an empty equipment van might be what both of us need.

Austin grins, clearly following my train of thought, but he shakes his head.

"You can still win this," he says, holding my hands between his. "All of it. Listen to Ivan. Stay focused. We've got time for everything else after."

Do we, though? Today has been a marathon, but we're literally mid-season. When the Olympics are over, we're off to Switzerland. Or is it Austria? Either way, the World Cup has four more meets this year. There's always another race. Another destination.

Austin kisses my cheek, brushing his fingers along my jaw. His hands are cold and I shiver.

"I'll see you after," he says. "Ski hard."

Then he turns and walks to the equipment tent where his final pair of skis for the afternoon are waiting.

I don't hear how he does in the Small Final. In fact, I tell Kage and Ivan I don't want anyone to tell me. I stand with my back to the starting area and all the other athletes, hands in front of me as I play out the course I will now never forget in my lifetime through my mind one last time. Start. Rollers, jump. Turn. Chicane. Jump. Over and over, with my hands in front of me, taking me to the end. To gold.

We assemble in the gate. It's like the semifinal, with Kage and me on opposite ends. The German skier is beside Kage. An American stands beside me.

"Good luck," he says, the first competitor who has spoken to me all day. I can only manage a tight smile in reply as I grip the handles and get ready for release.

My start is perfect. I might as well be on a string attached to the barrier that launches me forward as it falls. Someone grunts and swears before I'm even through the rollers. Did he fall? It happens. A fall in the start gate is the worst way to lose a race. There's no chance of coming back from that. No one wants their day to end like that, especially not in a final.

Jump, first turn. Someone's on my shoulder. The German. His next jump is better than mine, setting him up for the right line into the next turn that ends uphill. I have no choice but to let him take the lead. The only other option is to take us both down. But I only give him what the rules require and stay right on his tail as he goes for the chicane. Someone's close behind me too, tucked in close enough to draft. Kage, maybe? Or was it Kage who fell at the start?

We're airborne over the next jump. The German goes late and even though I took off after, I land first. He's still downhill of me, but the gap is closing. My thighs scream at me as I cling to control by the finest margin around the next turn. If we don't go too high, I can pass him. I tuck my arms in close, focusing on the moment, whether it's a bump or a lapse in concentration that will give me the opportunity I need to get by.

It comes as we round the last curve before the final pitch. The bells and whistles are going wild at the bottom, and for the tiniest moment, the German leans a little too far to the side. He has to dig in his edges to keep his skis from sliding out from under him, and that's all the chance I need. I point my skis down the slope and slip past him. He disappears from my peripheral vision so fast he might as well vanish and then I'm clear. Nothing between me and the last fifty metres to close before I cross the finish line.

I don't hear anyone coming before a blur of red and grey shoots past me like a rocket. He's moving so fast he must have been thrown from something. Kage flies by me tucked into the tightest ball imaginable and with only one target. The finish line.

In first place.

It's too late. All of this happens in a matter of seconds, and before I can even think of a way to respond to his challenge, we're over the line, amidst the throng of cheering fans. The world spins wildly and for the first time all day, I take a breath that I can feel all the way to my toes.

What happened? *How* did it happen?

But before I can even look for him, Kage charges at me, throwing his arms around me like he did in the tent. He laughs and screams and his excitement takes hold of me.

We won.

Gold and silver. Canada at the top of the podium.

It's not the perfect ending I imagined. Kage isn't Austin. But his victory cry and the answering calls from the Canadian fans is enough to wipe any regret from my mind for now.

We won.

We're engulfed in cheers. The German who came third. The American who had the poor luck to fall when it counted most. Matthieu. Ivan. My mom and dad. Two men who I've seen before and finally remember are Kage's two dads. I'm not even sure civilians are allowed in the finish area, but no one stops them. It's controlled pandemonium.

Then Austin's there, at the edge of my vision, hovering beyond the crowd. I fight my way through the people, accepting slaps on the back and congratulations offered without ever stopping to engage anyone. In this moment, possibly the biggest moment of my life so far, I only have eyes for Austin.

I stop when we're a few inches apart. No one has noticed me slip away. Someone's hoisted Kage onto their shoulders and he leads the crowd in another round of cheering and celebration. I hope, after everything, his is the story that makes the headlines tomorrow. Who needs clicks from gawkers who want the gossip about queer ski crossers when you can tell the whole country about the twenty-year-old barely out of junior racing who is now an Olympic gold medalist?

"You did it," Austin says, voice warm.

I can't help my smile. "Yeah. I did. How about you?"

He smiles too. And he doesn't ask why I don't know the result of his race. Austin gets it. Always has. There's no one I would want to spend this career with. This wild and dangerous ski life. No matter what risks lie ahead . . . what accidents and injuries lurk in the woods . . . he will always be there and he will understand.

"I came fifth," he says. Fifth. First in the Small Final. On any other day, he'd have been right up there with me and Kage.

He knows what I'm thinking and his grin widens.

"You're lucky I wasn't in the Big Final. I'd have mopped the floor with both of you."

"I'd like to see you try," I say, closing the space between us.

"Just wait," he says, tugging at my bottom lip between his teeth. "In four years, you'll eat my snow."

"That's what you think. You'll probably fall in the starting gate."

He laughs and I kiss him. This is it. My ending. My gold medal. Until the next race. The next mountain. In this brief moment between the highs of the sport we have chased our whole lives together, the only thing I need or want is Austin. In my life, in my arms, in my bed.

Falling is part of skiing, and falling for him is the easiest thing I've ever done.

―――――

Thank you for reading Ski-Crossed Lovers. For more adventures at the gayest games ever, check out A Good Puck, the next book in Love On The Podium.

ABOUT THE AUTHOR

Allison lives in Toronto with her very patient husband and the world's cutest team of rescue pets. She tries to split her time between writing, exploring Toronto's parks, and traveling anywhere that has good wine. Tragically, this leaves no time to clean the house.

LGBTQ+ ROMANCES BY ALLISON TEMPLE

Out & About

Work-Love Balance

Honeymoon Sweet

The Seacroft Series

Top Shelf

Cold Pressed

Hot Potato

Shared Series

My Not-So-Super Blind Date (part of Subparheroes)

Under Her Roof (part of Accidentally Undercover)

Puppuccino (part of Bold Brew)

Standalone

Destination Bedding

The Neighbourly Thing

Up North

Boyfriend With Benefits

The Pick Up

LGBTQ+ FANTASY BY ALLI TEMPLE

Afterlife Incorporated

Only Mostly Dead

Hate To Haunt You

Vacation From Hell (coming in 2026)

The Pirate & Her Princess

Uncharted

Unbroken

Unleashed